Suspended Entanglement

Suspended Entanglement

THE PAST LIFE PRISM SERIES
BOOK FIVE

JULIE BAWDEN-DAVIS

Roses
A R E
RED
PUBLISHING

ISBN-978-1-955265-45-4

ISBN-1-955265-45-3

Distributed by Roses Are Red Publishing

rosesareredpublishing.com

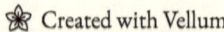 Created with Vellum

Acknowledgments

As they say, it takes a village. Here's my village. I'm supremely grateful to each of these fabulous people!

ARC Reading Gems
Kery Bailey
Julie Schlueter
Monte Bawden
Susa Fraccaroli
Trish Darrenkamp
Marilyn Smith
Lisa Starkey
Beth Helm
Chelle Young
Jacquelyn Gray
Ellen Ocean
Heather Wamboldt
MelK
Amber Mancebo
Pamela Bloink
Debb
Pros

Judy Bullard, cover design
Kyle Kane, Roses are Red logo design
Kery Bailey, Prism logo design
Sabrina Wildermuth, design consultation

Dedication

To second chance lifetimes and new beginnings.

Suspended Entanglement

THE PAST LIFE PRISM SERIES
BOOK FIVE

JULIE BAWDEN-DAVIS

Roses
A R E
RED
PUBLISHING

Prologue - North Vietnam, August 1972

The mosquitoes feasted on him in the dark, humid night. He smashed one on his shoulder just as it pierced his skin, then grasped the bamboo cage in both hands and went back to gnawing. A tooth had loosened on the right side of his mouth, so he used the left now.

Except for the sound of crickets, the air was quiet. A relief after a day of unrelenting heat punctuated by explosions. The warm water engulfed his feet and calves—offering safety from insect bites—yet inviting something much worse. Water vipers, ready to slither in and strike with their fangs delivering slow, painful death.

The Viet Cong would be here at first light to submerge him again, so he had to hurry if he wanted to get out before dawn. This time, he would make sure to camouflage himself better when he ran for the border.

A sharp pain stabbed his mouth. He stopped to pull a splinter from his gums, the metallic taste of blood covering his tongue. A vision of losing his first tooth as a kid flashed into his mind. He shook the memory out of his head immediately. Soft thoughts here got you killed.

He went back to chewing the cage, stopping when he heard a

sound nearby. Was it an animal, or worse, a human? He stood stock-still, glad for the cover of dark sky, the moon a mere sliver. If they caught him escaping again, it would be his last time. When he heard nothing more, he went back to work. Another couple of hours and he should be able to break himself free.

Chapter One - Present Day

Sophia was dreaming. She knew she was dreaming, and yet she didn't know. What she did know was that she was in Ryan's arms waltzing to Strauss's Blue Danube. Oh, how wonderful she felt. So free as he swung her around and they mirrored one another's steps. She almost felt as if she could fly.

It was then she saw her standing in the shadows of the great room, and that caused her to falter on her feet. So much so that Ryan had to catch her. When she looked back, she was gone, but as the waltz continued, she couldn't seem to regain the same carefree footing. Ryan had a concerned look in his eyes and murmured to her, "Pearl, is there something wrong?"

Should she tell him she had seen her? Or was it best she left things alone?

All eyes gazed upon them now as the orchestra finished—the star couple of the night.

"It's nothing Clifton," she said, then curtseyed for the onlookers, whose applause rose to the castle's lofty ceiling. The attention and adoration should have enlivened her, but she only felt dread.

Sophia shot up in bed and gasped, putting her hand to her

heart, thumping about in her chest. She looked at the bedside clock, unable to focus at first. Finally, the hour revealed itself—3:33 a.m. After calculating the time in Greece to be early afternoon, she pulled open her bedside drawer, took out her phone and powered it on, then pressed her grandmother's number.

"Little love, it's the middle of the night there. Is something wrong?"

"Grandmother, no, everyone is fine," Sophia started. "I—."

"A bad dream?"

"I'm not sure. It seemed to be something different than a dream. I'd call it a vision."

"Tell me what occurred."

Sophia closed her eyes. "It's so odd. It was as if I knew I was dreaming."

"So, a lucid dream, then," said her grandmother.

"I've heard of them. They are when you know you're dreaming, right?"

"Yes. Many say they are dreams you create as you go along. Others, such as I, believe they aren't really dreams, but instead you've stepped into an altered universe and are experiencing something that has occurred in the past or may occur in the future, or is even occurring concurrently."

Sophia struggled to digest what her grandmother had just said.

"Are you there, little love?"

"Yes, I'm just trying to understand all of this."

"You need some grounding. Why don't you get a drink of water. That will make you feel better."

"Okay," said Sophia as she got out of bed and made her way to the kitchen in her condo, quiet as Teddy slept down the hall. She filled a glass and drank several long gulps, then set it on the counter and glanced around. Her eyes seemed to be focusing better.

"Feeling more yourself now?" asked her grandmother.

"I am, thank you. So, from what I think you are saying, I must have been seeing something that occurred in a past lifetime with Ryan. But in that lifetime he was named Clifton, and I was Pearl. We were dancing in a castle, and many people were watching. It was a celebration of some sort."

"I believe it was your engagement party," said her grandmother.

Sophia thought for a moment. "That feels right."

"What was the trouble? I sense concern in your voice."

"At first, it was wonderful. I was floating above the dance floor as I waltzed with Ryan. But then something odd happened." Sophia stopped and swallowed.

"Go on."

"I saw a woman in the shadows in the crowd."

"Who was it?"

"I honestly don't know. It was as if I knew at that time, but I don't know now. Does that make any sense?"

"It makes perfect sense. It isn't time for you to know; otherwise, you would," said her grandmother.

"But it was very ominous and didn't feel good at all to see her."

"I understand. More will be revealed."

"That's all?" asked Sophia, exasperated.

"This is the way it works sometimes. You know that. What is really troubling you about this?"

Sophia sighed. "A couple of things. First, that I was dancing with Ryan, and it felt so wonderful."

Her grandmother laughed.

"What's so funny about that?"

"You're dancing with a handsome man and happy and you are troubled by this?"

"I..."

"There is no need to feel as if you are betraying Phillip. Didn't he tell you the same?"

"Yes, but…"

"Yes, but what? You can be happy with more than one man, I assure you."

"It all seems so—I don't know, clandestine."

Her grandmother chuckled. "Well, clandestine can be good at times."

"Grandmother!"

"What else is troubling you about your dream?"

"The woman I saw. I have a feeling she meant me harm. She had a dark heaviness about her."

"That is worrisome, but as I mentioned, more will be revealed when it is time. I feel a third concern. Are you worried that Phillip was also in that lifetime? I'm not seeing that he was."

Sophia ran a finger along the grout in between the tiles on her kitchen island. "Well, that's a relief. It's bad enough I'm cavorting with Ryan in that lifetime."

Her grandmother laughed again. "I sometimes wonder how you became so conventional."

"That's such a bad thing?"

"It isn't necessarily but I think you're going to need to let go of some of that in the coming months, Sophia."

"When you call me Sophia, I know I'm getting a lecture, Grandmother." She heard a bell clang on the other end of the line, signaling that her grandmother had a client. "We'll table this for now. Thank you for answering my call."

"I do hope I helped," said her grandmother.

"You did. Have a good session. I love you."

"And I love you."

Sophia hung up the phone and looked at the clock on the stove. It was a little past four a.m. now. As awake as she felt, she couldn't imagine being able to go back to sleep.

"That was quite a phone conversation," said Phillip, suddenly materializing.

"You heard it all?" she said to the wavery figure across the kitchen island.

"I did."

"Was my grandmother correct saying that you're okay with me and Ryan? If there is a me and Ryan, that is."

"I've already given you my blessing. And I thought he was coming over tonight for dinner?"

"He is. Please tell me you won't be here. I can't handle that."

Phillip chuckled. "I'll make myself scarce. I promise."

"I don't know that I can do this, Phillip."

"What? Open your heart to another?"

"Yes, no. I mean, I don't know if this is anything more than a friendship with Ryan."

"Oh, it is more than a friendship. I assure you."

"But it feels so odd talking to you about this."

"Mom?" said Teddy, who had appeared in the kitchen suddenly. "What's up? Everything okay?"

Sophia gripped the edge of the counter to steady herself. "Everything is fine. I'm sorry I woke you."

Teddy looked around. "Are you talking to Dad?"

She nodded.

"Can he see me and hear me?"

"Of course."

"Can you ask him something for me?"

"Certainly."

"Will I ace the trig test today, because I really need to."

Sophia laughed, easing the tension in her chest.

"What's so funny? And what does Dad say?"

"Tell him he'll do fine. He's got my head for numbers."

"He says you're going to do fine—because you take after him when it comes to math."

Teddy looked visibly relieved. "Thank him for me."

"He heard you. Why don't you try getting some more sleep?"

Teddy yawned and nodded, then shuffled back to his bedroom.

"Please tell me that he will do well today," she said.

"He's going to do fine. It's mind over matter, anyway. Maybe you should try to get some sleep, too."

"I don't know that I can sleep, but it would be good to try," said Sophia, who went back into her bedroom and climbed into bed, expecting to lay there wide awake, but soon found herself drifting off into a thankfully dreamless sleep.

Chapter Two

Sophia awoke to the sound of rain splattering her bedroom window. She glanced at the time. Past nine. Remembering her appointment at ten that morning with her new past life client, she jumped out of bed. Though she had a short commute to work, it was going to take longer than usual with the rain.

Twenty minutes later, she rushed up to Kline Counseling Center and reached to open the door. As she struggled to get inside without soaking herself and her briefcase, the door suddenly swung open. There stood Cathy, a cup of coffee in hand.

"Finally, the rainstorm they've been promising since Christmas," she said as Sophia hurried inside. "I guess a month late isn't so bad for Southern California."

After sliding her umbrella into the bucket by the door, Sophia peered out at the parking lot, now battered with driving sheets of rain. "It is coming down hard."

Cathy chuckled. "When we were kids whenever it rained, Phillip blasted 'It Never Rains in Southern California.' Drove my parents nuts. But you've got to admit, the song is spot on. When it finally gets going here, it sure does pour."

Sophia laughed. "He played that once when we were on our way to the beach in the rain."

"That sounds like Phillip. So, what's on the schedule today?"

"Gerald Walker is coming in," said Sophia.

"Oh, good. It'll be great for him to get over his fear of snakes."

Sophia went to the coffee machine and poured herself a cup. "I hope I can help him."

"I have complete faith in your ability to help him." Cathy nodded at the coffee cup Sophia held. "I thought you usually drank your own brew. As I recall, you don't like ours too much."

Sophia shook her head. "I slept in and was in a mad rush."

"Late night?"

Sophia took a sip and grimaced. "Not exactly. I had an unsettling dream that woke me up in the middle of the night. I called my grandmother to help me decipher it."

"That sounds disturbing."

Sophia thought about how the dream was about her and Ryan and wished she hadn't said anything. "I just needed some reassurance and explanation from my grandmother."

"Did talking to her give you some direction?"

Sophia nodded. "It turns out I was having a lucid dream."

"I remember learning about them back in college. They are dreams we are directing, if I remember correctly."

Sophia glanced at the clock on the wall. Gerald would be there any minute.

"According to my grandmother, that is one theory. The other is that what you are seeing is coming from a past or future lifetime. And something about an altered universe."

"Oh, my, that is a lot for a rainy Monday morning. I'll let you sort that out."

Sophia laughed as they both made their ways down the hallway to their respective offices.

Once in her space, Sophia flipped on the overhead light and fountain that sat along the wall. Just as she set her belongings on her desk, the front door chimed. That must be Gerald.

When she entered the waiting room to greet him, he closed his umbrella and set it in the bucket, then brushed water droplets from his suit and held out his hand to shake Sophia's. "You must be Dr. Strand. I'm Gerald Walker."

As they shook, she was momentarily jolted by a vision of him standing in a wooden cell, his chest bare and scarred. "It's so nice to meet you, Gerald," she said. "Would you like a cup of coffee before we head back to my office?"

He smiled then, his dark eyes lighting up. He was a tall man, who looked to be in his forties, with salt and pepper hair and a beard. Though he possessed an imposing presence that commanded attention, he had a gentle air about him.

"I already drank a pot today, so probably best to decline, although some water would be nice," he said.

Sophia poured him a cup, and they went back to her office and got settled, with Gerald sitting in the chair across from her desk.

"Cathy shared your history with me, in particular your ophidiophobia. I think she explained to you that I do past life regression therapy, which can help alleviate challenging situations in this lifetime."

Gerald loosened his tie. "Yes, she did explain it to me. My mother believed in reincarnation, so I have some knowledge of the subject. As Cathy must have told you, nothing has helped me get past this irrational fear of snakes."

"Interesting you should say irrational. It is often irrational thoughts and actions that point to a problem originating in a past life. May I ask what you do for work?"

Gerald sighed. "This is where things get embarrassing, and why I really need to get this under control. I'm a motivational speaker. Believe it or not, I teach people to conquer their fears and live their best lives. I've even written several books."

"Cathy did mention you are a public figure and have quite a following," said Sophia.

"So, you can see my problem. If anyone were to find out I'm

deathly afraid of a reptile, I don't know what that would do to my reputation."

"I do see your problem. Let me ask what may seem like an odd question. Have you ever been imprisoned?"

Gerald did a doubletake. "No, never. I don't even have speeding tickets. Why?"

Sophia framed her response carefully. "As part of my therapy, I will often see brief flashes of a person. The flashes are usually of past lifetimes. When we shook hands in the waiting room, I saw you standing in a cage."

As she said this, Gerald's eyes widened. "That is so strange you should say that. Ever since I was a kid, I've had these weird dreams about being stuck in an underwater cage."

"I recall reading about how they used underwater cages during the Vietnam War," said Sophia.

"Are you suggesting that I was in the Vietnam War?"

"I am thinking a prisoner of war."

"But what does that have to do with my fear of snakes?"

"The only way to find out is to regress you. Before we proceed, I'm happy to answer any questions about the modality."

Gerald looked at a spot beyond Sophia for a time, as if trying to find the right words. After a few long moments, he said, "Forgive me if this sounds like a silly question. But just to make sure. I can't get stuck in a past lifetime, can I?"

Sophia held back a smile. "That's not as silly of a question as you might think. In fact, many clients ask me that. No, you can't get stuck in a past lifetime. I did have a situation where a client went into a deep meditative state for a while, but it was more because she was utterly exhausted from caring for a sick child."

"I fortunately don't have a sick child to attend to, but my business does sometimes give me sleepless nights."

Sophia considered her words for a moment before replying. "I'm not sure how much Cathy told you about the modality I use, but as it turns out, those areas of your life where you are having difficulty tend to improve once the issues presenting themselves from a past life are resolved. However, in all transparency, things often get worse before they get better."

Gerald smiled. "Given the fact I tell my readers and students just that, I am going to take it as a sign I'm on the right track."

Sophia gestured to the couch. "Go ahead and get comfortable, and we'll get started."

Gerald went over to the couch and sat down, then slid out of his loafers. "Should I lie down and close my eyes?"

"Yes, that generally works best. I usually put on the sound of light rain when I do the meditation that begins the journey to a past lifetime, but today we have the real thing outside," she said as thunder rumbled in the distance and rain began pounding the roof even harder.

When this occurred, Gerald tensed.

"Is everything okay?" asked Sophia as she sat down in her armchair facing the couch.

Gerald opened his eyes and turned to her. "It was the oddest thing. I generally have no problems with the rain, but when I heard the thunder, it was as if something shifted inside of me, and it doesn't feel good."

Sophia suddenly saw Gerald running through a field of rice paddies, lightning in the distance.

"I think you flashed to the past lifetime you'll soon be visiting. More will be revealed when I regress you. Are you ready?"

Doubt flashed in Gerald's eyes.

"You'll be fine. Remember you are visiting a past lifetime. It can't hurt you now physically. I am going to record our session, if that's okay with you. I find that hearing yourself helps."

Gerald's expression became determined. "That's fine, Dr. Strand. Take me back to wherever I need to go."

Chapter Three

"Take several deep breaths," said Sophia. "As you do so, let the air flow out your body, fingers and toes. Picture the air as gray or black as it leaves your body, taking all tension and anxiety from you. Breathing, breathing, breathing. The more you can relax and let your mind wander where it may, the better," she said, waiting while thunder rumbled outside, slightly rattling the windows. She watched Gerald closely to see if he would react, but he appeared calm.

"Now I want you to focus on your shoulders. Let them sink into the couch. Continue to breathe slow and steady, expunging all the tension from your body. We move onto your chest now. Let that relax, then the rest of your torso. Breathing, breathing, all tension slipping away."

Ten minutes later, Sophia had Gerald in a deep, meditative state. His expression was peaceful, and his chest rose and fell at a steady pace.

"Now you're going to take a journey back in time to the first place your subconscious wishes to show you," said Sophia. "You're heading down a path, and you can see in the distance a purple door. When you reach the door and pass through it, you will see yourself in a past lifetime. You have arrived at the door. Reach out and turn the handle and open it. Tell me what you see."

Sophia watched fascinated as Gerald's entire countenance quickly changed. Whereas before he was peaceful and assured, his body language now emitted fear and hesitation. "If I go through the door, I may never come back," he said, his voice hushed.

Sophia sat up and leaned forward to look more closely at him. "Please explain what you mean by you will never come back."

His brow furrowed. "They told me if I escaped again, they would slit my throat after cutting out my tongue and eyes."

"Who are you speaking of?"

"The Viet Cong."

"I want you to listen very carefully to me. You are about to enter a doorway that will take you to something that happened in the past. It will be as if you are watching a movie. Your own movie." She paused for a second to let the information sink in. "Do you understand what I am saying?"

Gerald was silent for a moment, then whimpered, "I want to make it back home to my mother and father, but I don't know if I can go on."

Sophia considered how to deal with this, as it was the first time she had a client in a regressive state before even walking through the purple door. She wondered about the wisdom of having him go on.

Just then, however, Gerald said, his voice resolute, "If you say this is in the past, then I will go through the door."

Had he come out of his meditative state? "If you are sure, Gerald," she replied.

The man smiled then, his face suddenly peaceful. "My name is Brock, not Gerald."

"Nice to meet you, Brock. Have you walked through the purple door?"

"I walked through a groovy purple door, yes."

Sophia blinked several times. Gerald's face had completely transformed. She saw a younger version of him. "Where are you right now, Brock?"

Gerald opened his eyes and turned to Sophia, a faraway expression on his face. "I'm tripping right now."

Sophia wasn't sure what to do with this. "Tripping? As in taking drugs?"

Gerald laughed. "Yeah, drugs. Liquid haze, to be exact."

He must be speaking about LSD, thought Sophia.

"What is the year?"

"It's 1972, man. Free love, free everything."

"What are you doing?" she asked.

"Just hanging out. About to get some loving in."

"Who are you with?"

He chuckled. "Not sure of her name. But she's totally groovy and into me."

Sophia wasn't sure why she asked the next question. "Are you totally into her?"

Gerald frowned then. "No. I mean, the sex is great, but..."

"But you wish you were with someone else?"

His expression became pained, and he nodded. "Cheryl's gone. She told me she couldn't deal with going to Canada."

"Why are you going to Canada?"

He closed his eyes and scowled. "I don't want to talk about that anymore. You're ruining my vibe, man."

"Where do you live?" Sophia asked him.

Gerald waved his hand. "Here and there."

"In what state and city?"

"In Frisco, of course."

"You mean San Francisco?"

He snorted. "You sound like a total square, man, but yeah."

"You haven't been drafted yet?"

Gerald sighed. "Like I said, you're a total downer, man. No, not yet. But most of my friends have been. It doesn't matter if I get called, though, because I'm not going. I'm all set to head north."

"You plan on heading into Canada if you are drafted?"

Gerald vigorously nodded. "You betcha."

"Do you know anyone who has done that?"

"Yeah, Troy, my pal from grade school. He said if I got called to find him."

Sophia noted the time. Their session was just about up. "There is no way you will go to Vietnam if called? You're certain?"

"Never."

"But what about leaving your family? Your mother and father?"

Gerald snorted. "My old man is a total square, and my mother doesn't give me the time of day. Although I will miss my brother and sister."

This confused Sophia, given what he had said at the beginning of the regression. Her phone pinged then, indicating it was time to bring him back.

"It's time to return to the present," she said. "I'm going to start counting back from twenty. When I reach one, you will walk back out the purple door and into the present."

Sophia waited, hoping that he wouldn't protest. When he didn't say anything, she had a zing of panic. Could a person get stuck on a drug high while under?

"Gerald, do you hear me? It's time to come back now." She watched as his countenance changed once again, back to the fearful person she originally saw.

"Thank you," he said then. "I think it's best I don't go through the purple door today. Maybe next time."

"Who am I speaking to?" asked Sophia.

"I'm Devan. Number 3587654."

Sophia shook her head slightly. "You are Devan, not Brock?"

"I don't know any Brock."

"What year is it?" asked Sophia as her phone pinged, indicating an end to their session.

"It's 1972."

"And you were drafted?"

"Yes."

None of this made sense, but she had to bring him back now. "Okay, Devan, I am going to start counting back from twenty. When I reach one, open the purple door and walk back into the present, January 2022 in Orange, California."

When Sophia got to one and told him to open the door to the now, she breathed a sigh of relief when he turned to her and opened his eyes, his face appearing normal once again. "That was an odd experience," he said, motioning to sit up.

"Go slowly, you might be a little dizzy," said Sophia, who waited for him to sit and take a few breaths before she continued. "We are a little over our hour, but while you were under, you accessed quite a bit, so I let it continue. I hope you don't have another appointment soon."

Gerald shook his head. "I cleared my schedule this morning, so I'm fine."

"Okay, good. Tell me what you remember from the regression."

"At first, it felt great to relax. You do an excellent guided meditation. I do them for the attendees at my seminars, so I know."

"Thank you. I'm glad that it helped you relax. What else do you remember?"

Gerald frowned. "This may sound crazy, but I think I was in some sort of drug house, and..." he trailed off.

"I believe sex was also involved," added Sophia.

Gerald smiled. "Okay, so I'm not imagining things." He looked at her phone, which she held in her hand. "Do we have time for me to listen to what I said?"

"Yes, but first, do the names Brock or Devan mean anything to you?"

"Devan, no, but I had an Uncle Brock. I never met him. He

was my father's brother and a hippy. When he was drafted into the Vietnam War, he deserted and went to Canada. But then he returned to the U.S."

Sophia gave Gerald a stunned look.

"Did I say something, Dr. Strand? Forgive the clichéd expression, but you look like you've seen a ghost."

Chapter Four

T his was a new turn of events Sophia hadn't yet experienced with the regressions. Was Gerald somehow accessing his uncle's lifetime?

"I think the only way to try to explain things is to play the recording," she told him.

"Please do, Dr. Strand."

When Gerald heard himself speaking at first in a frightened tone, he commented, "I sound pretty scared."

Sophia nodded. "I thought the same."

When Gerald became Brock, his eyes flew open. "What the— excuse my French—hell," he exclaimed.

Sophia stopped the recording. "Now you understand my shock a bit ago."

Gerald's brow furrowed. "I know I never talked to you about my uncle, so how did I come up with that?" He gestured to the phone.

"Is your uncle still alive?"

"No, he died before I was born."

"There's more, if you're ready," she said, resuming when he nodded in agreement.

When Brock mentioned free love, Gerald chuckled, then murmured, "I wonder who Cheryl is?"

At the end of the tape, he leaned back on the couch. "Well, I have to say, this is much different than I thought it would be."

"May I ask what you thought it would be?"

"I guess I don't really have a frame of reference, but I figured you'd put me under, find out where the fear of snakes came from, and then we'd work on an extraction of the fear process, or something along those lines."

Sophia thought for a moment about how to reply. "While that can sometimes happen, I've found that usually with the past life regression therapy it is somewhat of a meandering road to better, if that makes sense."

Gerald ran his hands through his beard. "That makes perfect sense. I tell my students the road to fulfillment is not a straight one."

"Another thing I've found with this treatment modality is that the pieces of the puzzle begin to put themselves in place with time, and more regressions."

Gerald put his hands on his knees and motioned to stand up. "Well, I'm ready to schedule my next session, Dr. Strand."

Sophia went to her calendar. "How soon would you like to come back?"

"I'm thinking the sooner the better. Now that we've opened this past life with Brock, I'm curious to see what happened, and of course, deal with my fear of snakes."

"How about tomorrow morning at 10 a.m.?"

"Perfect. Thank you for everything. I appreciate your knowledge and guidance on this."

Sophia walked him out and watched as he headed toward his car in the parking lot. The rain had subsided, and it just sprinkled now. As he reached for his car door handle, a young woman with long, flowing black hair appeared and touched his arm, then disappeared.

. . .

Sophia had two more of what she considered traditional clients in the early afternoon, and then packed her things up quickly so she could get to the grocery store. She had promised Ryan a three-course meal, and she wanted to make dinner as delicious as possible.

"Perhaps roasted chicken and asparagus risotto," said Phillip suddenly.

"You know, it's a bit off putting when you do that," said Sophia as she turned off the lights in her office.

"What, materialize suddenly or read your mind?"

"Both, and what happened to you making yourself scarce when Ryan comes over?" Sophia still felt uncomfortable about this on so many levels.

"I thought we were talking about when he comes over tonight. This is just about what you're making for dinner."

Sophia sighed.

"Not this again. I'm perfectly fine with you and Ryan. More than fine, actually."

Sophia glanced at her bookshelf, the book *Many Lives, Many Masters* seeming to jump out at her. "And why are you so fine with it? Tell me?"

"You know I love you more than anything but you can be obtuse at times."

Sophia gave a wry laugh. "How so?"

"I wish for you to be happy is the main reason. And I know that if you give Ryan a chance, he can make you happy. Besides, it's his turn, in terms of past lifetimes."

"What does that mean?"

Silence. Phillip had disappeared.

Sophia started to walk out of her office when her phone pinged. She checked the screen. A text from Teddy. *I hope you're not still at work, Mom. You need to get ready for your big date tonight. What are you cooking? Please tell me something super gourmet that will totally impress Professor Collins.*

Sophia chuckled and replied. *No worries, Teddy, I'm just*

leaving the office and on my way to the grocery store. I'm thinking roasted chicken and red potatoes, and asparagus risotto.

Teddy immediately sent back a thumbs up and a smiley face.

"Teddy, what are you doing up?" asked Sophia as she turned on her bedside lamp, noting that it was 3 a.m.

Ten years old at the time, her son stood in the doorway of her bedroom, an odd expression on his face.

"Did you want to come in and lie down?" she asked him.

"I'm too old to sleep with you," he said, his thick hair mussed, a frown on his face.

Sophia got out of bed and went to stand in front of him. "What's the matter, honey? Do you not feel well?"

Teddy shook his head. "I'm fine."

"You don't look fine, and you're up at 3 in the morning. What gives?"

Teddy opened his mouth to speak, then shut it again. Sophia let the silence settle between them. If she gave him some time, he generally talked.

"Do you want to go get a drink of water?" she asked after several moments of silence.

Teddy shook his head.

"I can't help you if you don't talk to me."

"That's just it," said Teddy, his eyes beginning to glisten with tears he was obviously trying mightily to hold back. "I don't want to talk to you."

"Teddy," Sophia started.

Teddy brushed his hands over his face. "I'm sorry, Mom, that's not what I meant. I just meant..." he trailed off.

"That you want to talk to your father, is that it?" she asked softly.

In answer, tears began sliding down his face, and he nodded.

Sophia pulled her son to her as he sobbed, her heart aching. How she so wished that Phillip was there to talk to his son, too. When his crying subsided and he pulled back to look at her, Sophia said, "I know I'm not your father, but if you want to talk about it, we can. Perhaps over some cocoa?"

Teddy, always so sunny, gave her a small smile. "That sounds good."

In the kitchen, he sat down on a stool at the island while Sophia heated up milk and added cocoa and sugar to the pan. She was quiet while she did so, knowing that her son needed a minute or two to get his thoughts together.

When she put the hot cocoa in front of him and pulled up a stool with hers in hand, he finally opened up.

"There's this guy at school. His name is Peter."

Sophia nodded for him to continue.

"He's mean. A real ass." Teddy stopped to see if his mother would react to his cussing, but she let it slide.

"Is he bullying you, is that it?"

Teddy shook his head. "No, he's bullying this other kid named Carl. Everyone thinks it's funny."

"But you don't."

"No, it's terrible. I feel so bad for the guy. I tried to talk to him, but he is so freaked out about being bullied that he's afraid of me, too." Teddy took a sip of cocoa. "I know this is something that you and I could talk about, but they're making fun of him in the locker room, and..." Teddy trailed off.

Sophia sat up straighter. "Oh, I see."

"So, what should I do, Mom? If I tell the teacher, I think it's only going to make things worse for Carl, especially in the locker room."

"You're probably right," said Sophia, unsure of how to guide her son with this conundrum. She'd never been in a men's locker room, so she could only imagine what the other boys were saying to Carl.

As she struggled to find a response, she felt as if someone whispered in her ear what she then suggested. "What about if you invite him over after school? That way you'll be away from all the other kids, and it'll give you a chance to get to know each other. Soon enough, he'll see that he doesn't have anything to fear from you. I'm sure he's very lonely."

Teddy nodded slowly. "I think that's a great idea, Mom. I'll do it tomorrow."

"I'm glad I could help," said Sophia, her heart warming at the smile on her son's face.

Chapter Five

Sophia dashed through the doors of Albertsons just as the sky let loose and rain began pounding the parking lot. Shivering as she grabbed a cart, she pulled out her phone and glanced at the time. She'd have to hurry if she was going to get dinner in the oven on time.

For the next fifteen minutes, Sophia hurried through the store. She was glad to see they had asparagus in stock, as well as baby red potatoes. After locating a perfect sized roasting chicken, she went to get rice for risotto. As she headed for check out, she remembered they had finished the last bottle of wine when Professor Kirten was over recently, so she went to the liquor section and chose a pinot grigio from a Northern California vineyard.

At home a few minutes later as she got to work in the kitchen, she noticed how quiet the condo seemed.

"Looks like you're being true to your word and making yourself scarce, Phillip," she murmured as she put the chicken in the oven and set the temperature.

That done, she cleaned the potatoes, which she planned on roasting in garlic and olive oil. After sliding them into the oven, she got to work on the risotto.

When all the food was cooking, she rushed to her room to get ready, grimacing when she opened the closet. What to wear? She, of course, wanted to look nice, but dinner at her house didn't call for formal. After fifteen minutes of sorting through outfit after outfit, she decided on a mauve skirt and white sweater. Then she ran a brush through her hair and put on some makeup and the pearl earrings her mother had given her when she graduated from high school.

She was checking out her reflection in the mirror when her phone pinged. A text from Teddy. *I'm going to dinner and the movies with Cerise. Good luck with your date!*

At exactly seven, the doorbell rang. Sophia took a deep breath and went to answer it, her heart flip-flopping when she came face-to-face with Ryan. He looked handsome and fresh-scrubbed in a green polo shirt and khaki slacks; his hair wet from the rain.

"Come in out of the wet," she said.

He walked in and pulled her to him for a kiss, his surprise move making her heart beat even faster.

When they finished, she said, "It's very nice to see you, too."

A twinkle in his eye, Ryan replied, "I've been thinking about our kiss at school. I wanted to make sure it wasn't a dream."

Sophia, who rarely giggled, found herself doing so. Then she noticed a small box in his hands. "Is that for me?"

He handed it to her. "Just a little something." Then he inhaled and said, "Something smells delicious."

Sophia led him to the kitchen, where she opened the refrigerator and pulled out the bottle of wine. "No rain jacket or umbrella for you?" she asked.

"Didn't you know it doesn't rain in Southern California?"

Sophia laughed. "As I recall, the song does mention that it pours." She handed him the wine bottle. "Speaking of pouring."

"I'll be happy to do the honors if you can point me to your wine opener."

"Second drawer from the refrigerator," she said as she went to check the potatoes, which looked to be done. As she pulled them out and set them on top of the stove, she heard the cork come loose.

Ryan held up the bottle. "Glasses? Or shall we drink straight from the bottle?"

As he said this, she had a brief flash of him in another lifetime. He wore a tux, and had his hair slicked back, his tie a bit askew, a champagne bottle in one hand. Taken aback by the vision, she turned and opened a cupboard, pointing to stemware on the top shelf. She moved aside so that Ryan could take down two wine glasses, which he set on the counter and began filling.

He handed her a glass, then held his up. "What shall we toast to?"

Sophia frowned. "About me standing you up at the Hobbit. I just want to say again how sorry I am."

Ryan met her eyes. "No need to rehash that. It's all water under the bridge. How about we toast to fresh starts?"

Sophia clinked her glass with his. "To fresh starts."

After they had both taken a sip, she remembered the box he had given her. She picked it up from the counter where she had set it. "You've piqued my curiosity. I'm going to open this now."

"It's just a little something," said Ryan as she lifted the lid.

Inside lay a small kitten figurine. She pulled it out of the box. "How precious. Thank you."

"I'm not sure what made me buy it for you. I don't recall you telling me you had pets, but I felt like you needed a kitten. Of course, this one you don't have to feed or bring to the vet."

Sophia laughed. "It's funny you should say that. I've been thinking lately about getting a kitten for company now that Teddy is getting ready to go off to college. I know he'll still be living at home initially, but he's not here much nowadays." Then she added quickly, "As it should be."

"Well, then, you can try this kitty on for size," said Ryan, who pulled up a stool at the island. "How was your day today? Busy at work?"

Sophia flashed to Gerald's session. "It was a bit hectic."

Ryan picked up the saltshaker and put it back down. "I guess that will happen with your line of work."

Sophia took a sip of wine, wondering how much she should tell him about her work. As she was swallowing, she heard a woman's voice whisper in her ear, *Just tell him what you do, my dear. I assure you he will be interested in the past life work.* At the sound of the unfamiliar voice, Sophia choked on the wine and began madly coughing.

"Are you okay?" asked Ryan.

Sophia nodded as she continued to cough, finally managing to say, "The wine just went down the wrong pipe."

Ryan stood up. "Let me get you some water."

As he filled a glass for her, Sophia's mind raced as to who could have been speaking to her. When he handed her the water and she took several long sips, the coughing finally subsided.

Ryan smiled. "Better now?"

"Yes, thank you." She was considering how she might broach the subject of her past life treatments with him when the oven buzzer went off, signaling that dinner was ready.

"Saved by the bell," said the voice.

Chapter Six

Sophia shut the cupboard and put the last dish away when the front door opened and shut, and Teddy came bursting into the kitchen.

"So, how was it?"

Sophia ran the dishtowel over the countertop. "It was really nice."

Teddy's eyebrows rose. "Really nice? Like how nice?"

"Teddy."

"I'm not trying to pry, Mom. I'm just curious." He went to the refrigerator and pulled open the door, then lifted the lid on the chicken. "Did Professor Collins like the food?"

"You can call him Ryan, and he did enjoy the meal."

Teddy pulled the chicken out of the fridge and set it on the counter, then took a plate from the cupboard.

"I thought you ate with Cerise?"

"I did, but this looks really good." He began piling chicken on the plate. "So, tell me all about your date."

Sophia chuckled.

Teddy, who had shoveled a mouthful in, said between bites, "What's so funny? Just give me the highlights. Did he ask you out again?"

"He did, as a matter of fact. Saturday we're going to the Getty."

"That's cool. What else happened?"

Sophia thought about the rest of the evening with Ryan. How they talked for a good two hours about everything and anything. She greatly enjoyed hearing his stories about growing up in Wisconsin and roaming the nearby mountain range as a kid and camping out on his own. She shared with him what it was like to grow up in Northern California, and how she loved the vineyards. They didn't talk much about her work, so the opportunity to tell him about the past life regression therapy didn't come up again.

"Mom?" said Teddy, grinning. "Was it that good? You're not saying anything."

Sophia faked a yawn. "Sorry, just tired. It's been a long day."

Teddy set down his fork. "Please, I'm dying here. Just give me a brief overview."

"As I already said, we had a very nice time. We talked about our childhoods and how he likes living here in Orange and teaching at the university. It was a lovely night, and I look forward to seeing him again. How's that?"

Teddy shrugged. "That'll have to do. I'm not going to ask if he kissed you goodnight."

Sophia swung around before Teddy could see the goofy grin on her face. Ryan had kissed her goodnight, alright. She could still feel his lips on hers.

"Good night, Teddy," she called over her shoulder as she headed down the hallway. "Make sure to clean up after yourself." Then she closed her bedroom door and floated to the bathroom to get ready for bed.

The next day dawned bright and clear. No more rain forecasted, Sophia noted as she sat in the kitchen sipping coffee while checking the weather on her phone. Teddy had left early, so she was alone in the house. She dialed a familiar number and waited.

"Little love, how are you doing this morning?"

"I'm doing well, Grandmother. How was your day? I hope I didn't interrupt your dinner."

"I've eaten and am now digesting. It's always a pleasure to hear from you, but I sense some questions."

"First of all, I'm curious about something," said Sophia.

"And what is that?"

"How are you and Randall getting along?"

"Swimmingly. We talk every evening. Well, my evening and his morning, of course."

"I hope I'm not taking up his time spot," said Sophia.

"No, we've already spoken." She heard her grandmother chuckle under her breath. "I can hear you wondering when we'll be seeing each other again?"

Sophia laughed. "Yes, I'm curious."

"We're talking about taking a cruise through the Panama Canal over spring break when he has some time off from teaching."

Sophia smiled. "I'm so glad to hear that."

"Now that we've spoken of my matters of the heart, tell me all about yours. I understand from Teddy that you had your professor over for dinner last night?"

"My son certainly has a big mouth," said Sophia, exasperated.

"He means well, you know that," said her grandmother.

"I know, and I love him for it. The dinner date was lovely. However, something did occur that I wanted to talk to you about."

"Do tell."

"Ryan asked about my work, and I was thinking about telling him about the past life regressions when I heard a woman's voice whisper something in my ear. It wasn't your voice. I've never heard the voice before. What do you make of it?"

"First of all, what did the woman say?"

"That I should tell him about the past life work."

"So, you have finally accessed her," said her grandmother.

"Who? Do you know her?"

"I don't, but you do."

Sophia got up and took a banana from the fruit bowl. "How do I know her but you don't when I've never heard her voice before."

"You've heard *from* her many times throughout your lifetime. You just haven't heard her voice."

Sophia turned her grandmother's words over in her mind. "I'm not sure what you are saying."

"We have talked of life guides."

"Is she my life guide?"

"That's what I am telling you."

"But why haven't I noticed her before?"

"Because you weren't ready to. Though everyone has a life guide, many people aren't aware of that fact. It's uncommon to knowingly be guided by them."

"That seems odd. You would think being guided by your life guide would be useful."

"It is very useful, but a person has to be well-versed in hearing from the other side in order to hear from their life guide."

"Then what is the purpose of having one if most people don't hear them?" asked Sophia.

"Because they do guide you. You just aren't aware the guiding is going on. For instance, they will give you a nudge to avoid something or someone dangerous."

"Like an intuitive thought or gut feeling?" asked Sophia.

"Exactly. Your life guide has gotten you out of quite a few pickles over your lifetime, as has mine."

"Do you hear from your life guide?"

"I do. Ben talks to me quite frequently."

"He?"

"Yes, my life guide is a he, but as you heard, yours is female. It can vary."

"What should I do now that I've heard from her?"

"Start by finding out her name. And then ask what she would like you to know."

"Okay, I can do that," said Sophia, who glanced at the clock. She needed to get to the office for her session with Gerald.

"What else can I help you with?" asked her grandmother.

"Something odd happened with the regression I did yesterday. To be honest, I'm flummoxed."

"Tell me about it."

Sophia explained how Gerald regressed and was Brock, who happened to have the same name and story as his uncle, and then about Devan.

"Very interesting that this should occur," said her grandmother. "It's a rather advanced phenomenon."

"It certainly seems advanced. Can you explain it to me? I have a session with the man soon, and I'd like to go in somewhat enlightened."

"From what you've told me, Brock and Devan are the same person. It sounds like they were living parallel lives during the war. One half went to war and the other deserted."

"Why on earth would someone want to do that?"

"To learn different lessons simultaneously. It's like studying for two master's degrees at the same time."

"And what of this being similar to his uncle's lifetime?"

"It could be he is his uncle. Is his uncle still alive?"

"He said his uncle died before he was born. So, you're telling me he is his uncle?" Suddenly, Sophia felt terribly overwhelmed. "I am feeling so out of my league right now. This is a lot."

Her Grandmother laughed on the other end of the line. "Welcome to my world. It's always a lot. Just take one step at a time. You'll be fine. I promise."

"I hope so," said Sophia, wondering if this time she had taken on much more than she could handle.

Chapter Seven

S ophia had just opened the office and started brewing coffee when Gerald arrived. He appeared disheveled, as if he'd had a hectic morning.

"Dr. Strand," he greeted her, glancing at the coffee.

"Would you like some?" she asked.

"That would be great. I've had a rough morning."

Sophia poured him a cup. "Cream or sugar?"

"Thank you, I'll take it black." He reached out and took the coffee, then frowned. "I have a young fan. She was having a morning."

As he said this, Sophia noticed a slight blush on his face. She waited for him to go on, but instead he glanced around the room.

"How about we go into my office and we can discuss it?" she suggested.

When they had settled themselves, Sophia said, "You were saying about your young fan?"

Gerald set the coffee on the end table next to the couch. "Her name is May, and she needed my help this morning. I try to always keep things professional with my fans, but she has a way of pushing my boundaries, or I should say, I allow her to push my boundaries."

Sophia smiled. "That would be the enlightened way to look at the situation. The question is, why do you think you allow her to push your boundaries?"

Gerald looked at his hands, clasped in his lap, then at Sophia. "This is going to sound crazy, or maybe it won't, but I feel like we've known each other before."

"In past lifetimes?"

He nodded. "If it wasn't for my session yesterday, I wouldn't have caught it, but from the moment we first met at one of my seminars, I felt a connection."

"It is quite common for clients I help to have people in their lives who figure prominently in significant past lifetimes."

"So that could be the case, then?" he asked.

"Yes, most likely. Of course, the best way to find out is to regress you and see if May shows up as someone else."

Gerald lay back on the couch. "Let's do that. Hopefully along the way, we'll find out more about my fear of snakes."

Sophia turned on the sound of light rain and started the meditation.

Fifteen minutes later, Sophia had Gerald in a deep meditative state. "I'm going to have you walk down a pathway," she said softly. "At the end of the path, you will see a purple door. When you see it, turn the handle and enter."

Gerald's brow furrowed. "I don't see a purple door."

"What do you see?"

"I see a waterfall."

"Tell me about the waterfall."

"It's very large. I'm afraid if I approach too closely, I will be swallowed up by it."

Sophia thought for a moment, then asked, "Have you seen this waterfall before?"

He nodded, his expression becoming pained. "When I was running."

When he said nothing more after a few beats, Sophia asked, "Running from what?"

"The Viet Cong."

So, Gerald had somehow entered the past lifetime without going through the purple door, or perhaps it was already open, she thought.

"Are you running now?"

Gerald began to groan. "I am trying, but the bite on my leg is swelling and is terribly painful."

Sophia leaned forward. "What bit you on the leg, Gerald?"

"My name is not Gerald," he said, beads of sweat beginning to form on his brow.

"What is your name?"

"It's Devan."

"Okay, Devan, what bit you on the leg?"

"A snake when I was escaping the cage. I don't feel well from the bite." As he said this, Gerald began to breathe heavily.

"What's happening now, Devan?"

"They're coming for me, and the only way to get away from them is to jump into the waterfall."

Moments later when Gerald began hyperventilating, Sophia thought it best to bring him back.

"I want you to return to the present now," she said firmly. "You can go back at another time, but right now it's time to come back. I'm going to count backward from ten, nine, eight. Head back to the now. Seven, six, five, four. You are almost back to the now. Three, two, one. Open your eyes. You are back in Orange, 2022."

Sophia waited on the edge of her chair for Gerald to return. When his eyes flew open, he said, "I remember everything that just happened."

"You were talking about a waterfall and having been bitten. Tell me what you saw and how you felt."

Gerald sat up slowly and blinked a few times. "There was a giant waterfall, and I'm pretty sure I jumped into it because the Viet Cong were after me. But my leg was hurting something awful." He stopped for a moment, then his eyes lit up. "I think I was bitten by a snake. Is that where my fear of snakes comes from?"

"It's highly likely," she said.

He ran a hand through his hair. "I know this is going to sound strange, but I don't think I died in the waterfall. I can't imagine how I didn't die, because it was massive, but I don't think I did."

Sophia smiled. "Believe me, nothing sounds strange to me anymore when it comes to past lives. If you think you survived, you likely did."

"The question is how." Gerald glanced at the clock on the wall. "Do we have time for me to go back and find out?"

Sophia considered. "I brought you back because your breathing became labored. You appeared to be hyperventilating."

When Gerald frowned, she added, "But if you're feeling okay now—not too lightheaded or short of breath—we could try again. I must warn you, though, that you won't necessarily go back to where you just were. You may land in a different time in that lifetime, or even a different lifetime."

Gerald's expression became reflective. "I'm beginning to understand how this works. I remember reading once how there are quantum physicists who believe time is not chronological, but rather fluid, and that it can even move from past to present and back again, and that past and present can be occurring at once." He chuckled. "At the time, to be honest, I thought it sounded a bit like lunacy, but now..."

Sophia laughed. "Now it doesn't seem so crazy, or at least somewhat understandable?"

Gerald nodded. "Exactly."

"Are you ready to go under and test the time hypothesis?"

In answer, Gerald laid back down and closed his eyes.

Chapter Eight

This time, Sophia was able to get Gerald into a meditative state quickly, and when she asked him to look for the purple door, he readily found it.

"I'm in now," he said, his expression becoming pensive.

"Where are you?"

"We finished basic training last week, and now I'm in Vietnam on a helicopter at nighttime. They're going to put us down in the jungle. I'm nervous about using my parachute."

Devan held his breath, then reminded himself to breathe as the copter's blades slit the night. They had been warned enemy fire could occur, but so far it was quiet. He had checked his parachute multiple times and knew it to be ready. In moments, he and four other soldiers would plummet into the dark night, to hopefully find shelter until dawn when they would make their way to basecamp.

While part of Devan was terrified to jump out of the plane into the Vietnamese jungle, the other part of him was excited to finally soon have his boots on the ground. When the pilot signaled it was time to jump, he waited his turn, then plunged into the hollow darkness. Before long, he set down at the edge of a wetland, barely visible in the milky light of a crescent moon. Listening intently, he heard only the sound of crickets. Where were the other members of his team?

When her phone pinged, signaling it was time to end the session, Sophia said, "You need to come back now. You will be able to return at a later time, but right now you are needed in the present. I am going to count backward from twenty. When I get to one, you will open the purple door and step back into the present. Twenty, nineteen, eighteen, seventeen, sixteen, fifteen, fourteen, thirteen. You are almost back. Twelve, eleven, ten, nine, eight, seven, six, five, four, three, two, one. You are now back in Orange in January 2022."

When Gerald opened his eyes, he remained lying on the sofa looking up at the ceiling. She waited a moment for him to ground before speaking. "It looks like this time you were on a helicopter," she said.

Gerald sat up. "It was the night I arrived in Vietnam."

"You seemed excited," said Sophia.

"Like many unsuspecting young men back then." He shook his head. "It's funny when I think back now to learning about the Vietnam War in school. Even back then, I had a really bad feeling about it that made me feel anxious, which I never understood, until now."

"That is something that commonly occurs once you start accessing past lifetimes. You will begin to see patterns in terms of feelings you've had about certain time periods that you never understood before," said Sophia.

Gerald gave her a small smile. "If it wasn't me in the middle of what we now know was a brutal war in Vietnam, I would find this fascinating. Not that I don't find it interesting, but..." He stopped for a moment, then put his hand on his heart. "These regressions are much more emotionally charged than I ever imagined they would be. Is that normal?"

"It is quite normal," said Sophia just as her phone pinged, indicating their session had ended.

Gerald stood. "Thank you. I'd like to see you again tomorrow, if you have room in your schedule. With my seminar coming quickly, I really want to resolve things with this."

"Tomorrow at the same time is open," said Sophia, who didn't comment on things getting resolved quickly. From where she sat, there was still a lot more to be revealed for Gerald.

Sophia was making her way back to her office after walking Gerald out when she ran into Cathy in the hallway.

"I heard Gerald's voice. How are his sessions going?" asked Cathy, who held a cup of coffee in one hand.

"I'm not sure yet, but we have possibly uncovered the source of his fear of snakes. I know he has given me permission to discuss his case with you, so I can tell you he was badly bitten while running from the Viet Cong."

Cathy burst out laughing. "I am so glad I sent him to you. There is no way we would have accessed that with traditional therapy." She shook her head. "I continue to be amazed at the modality. And I have to say that it sounds like a movie I'd like to watch."

"Well, then, I can add that he appears to have jumped into a huge waterfall and survived, and that he was living a parallel life at the time as his uncle, a deserter who fled to Canada."

Cathy, who had just taken a sip of coffee, sputtered, "I would ask if you're kidding me, but I know you don't joke about clients. How is that even possible?"

Sophia shrugged. "I'm still trying to figure it out, but my grandmother says it's a thing."

"Phillip would have loved all this stuff. He was totally into quantum physics, as you know, and taught about it."

"I wish I had been able to take one of his physics classes. I think it would have shed some light on things for me now," said Sophia.

Cathy's eyebrows popped up. "I think I have the next best thing. I saved all his papers from his work at the college. I didn't have the heart to get rid of them. Chuck complains they're just collecting dust. You're welcome to come over and sort through things and see if you can find his class notes and syllabus and exams."

The thought of seeing and touching Phillip's teaching materials sent an excited feeling through Sophia. "I would love to. Thank you for thinking of it."

"Let's have you over for dinner this week, and you can take a look. What about Saturday?"

Sophia was about to reply yes but then remembered she had a date with Ryan.

When she hesitated, Cathy said, "Do you have other plans? Something with Teddy?"

Sophia thought about how to broach the topic of dating Ryan. "No, I..." she started.

Cathy waited expectantly, finally saying, "Look, if it's personal."

Sophia shook her head. "No, I need to tell you this. It's best you hear it from me. In November when my grandmother was visiting, I happened to be at the grocery store buying items for our dinner with Professor Kirten when I bumped into another professor at the university who knew Phillip." Sophia stopped talking and waited.

When Cathy got an ah-ha expression, she blurted, "Are you trying to tell me you are dating this professor?"

Sophia swallowed and nodded.

Cathy surprised her when she whooped. "I'm so happy to hear that."

"You are?"

"You and I both know it's well past time, Sophia. I know you loved my brother with all your heart and that you still love him, but he wouldn't want you to die a nun. What is his name? I wonder if I knew him or maybe Chuck knows of him."

"Ryan Collins. He teaches in a couple of the colleges—business administration and philosophy."

"That name does sound familiar," said Cathy, whose eyes lit up. "Tell you what. Why don't you see if he'd also like to come to dinner. Maybe Sunday? Chuck and I would love to meet the new man in your life, and he might be interested in seeing Phillip's notes." She frowned. "Unless you think that would be too awkward for you both?"

Sophia considered. "I think that would be fine. Phillip came up the first time we met."

"It's settled then. Talk to him and let me know."

Just then the front doorbell chimed. "That's my next client." Cathy winked at Sophia and headed to the waiting room.

As she bustled away, Sophia felt a wave of relief. She had been so anxious about telling her sister-in-law she had a man in her life other than Phillip, but it looked like her worry was for nothing.

Chapter Nine

"How is Cerise healing up?" asked Sophia that evening when she got home and found Teddy preparing to head out to visit her.

He stopped putting schoolbooks in his backpack. "Physically, she's a lot better. But she's still having flashbacks from the accident. Her mom and dad are having her see a therapist for PTSD symptoms. I thought maybe she could see you, but her mom already has a therapist because of what happened with her dad."

"That makes sense. I'm glad she's getting some help. The accident was pretty scary. I'm not surprised she's having flashbacks. Treatment sooner than later is best with PTSD."

Teddy's raised his eyebrows. "Oh, yeah? I guess it's good I talked her into it, then."

Sophia smiled. "I would expect nothing less from the son of a therapist. It would be nice to see her when she's up to coming for dinner one night."

Teddy zipped his backpack and slung it over his shoulder. "Speaking of dinner, I better get going. Her mom puts the meal on at six. I'll mention to Cerise coming over here. I'm sure she'd love that." He motioned to leave but stopped and looked at the floor. "I'm not sure how tonight is going to go. On Wednesdays, her dad joins for dinner."

"I'm sure that can be a bit tough," said Sophia. "Did you say he stopped the affair with the other woman?"

"He did, but Cerise's mom is still really angry. She tries to keep it inside, but it comes out. Like last week when she accidentally didn't make enough food. She said she didn't expect him to show up, even though he had shown up for the past three weeks every Wednesday."

"Resentment and pent-up anger are very common when it comes to infidelity on the part of the person who has been cheated on. I hope her parents can work past it, and I know Cerise hopes for it, but it isn't always possible when trust has been broken like that," said Sophia.

Teddy thought for a moment. "I can understand that. I would never cheat on Cerise, but if she cheated on me, even though I love her, I don't think I'd ever trust her again."

Sophia smiled. "From the way she looks at you, I don't think that is going to be an issue. You better get going."

When Teddy bustled out and slammed the door, the condo became silent as it always did in his wake. She went to the refrigerator and opened it to see a bit of leftover chicken. She'd heat that up with some veggies and potatoes and she'd be all set.

"I would never have cheated on you," said Phillip's voice then as he suddenly materialized.

Sophia took out the chicken and a head of broccoli and set them on the counter. "I know that about you. It's one of the many reasons I loved, I mean, love you."

"You don't have to apologize for using the past tense, my love. I know what you meant."

Sophia leaned against the kitchen island, suddenly feeling irritated. "Do you, really? Know what I mean? Sometimes I feel as if what I say to you doesn't resonate. Like you discount my concerns."

"Where is this coming from? Your date with Ryan? Did it not go well?"

Sophia looked up to see a wavy form across the island. "I would think you would know how my date went."

"I promised you I wouldn't eavesdrop, and I didn't, Sophia."

"My date went well."

"I'm glad to hear that. Now for what is bothering you. I think you know."

"I really have no idea. Enlighten me."

"The perfect family. Wasn't that a dream of yours as a girl?"

Sophia did a doubletake. "How do you know about that dream? I don't recall telling you."

"Let's just say we can see things from here. The present, of course, but also the past and future. Although we aren't often at liberty to discuss what will occur."

Sophia pulled out a stool and sat down. She stared at the salt-shakers she and Teddy bought at an art fair—two pigs with wings. They often joked about how their pigs could fly.

"I hear you thinking," said Phillip.

"Of course you do." Sophia took a deep breath. "Yes, I dreamed of the perfect family when I was young. Not so much me staying home behind the white picket fence, because I always imagined myself leaving the house to work and help people. But I did have a vision of children and a loving husband. That us against the world type of scenario I so wished for Teddy and did my best to create with him."

She put up a hand then to stop Phillip from replying and continued. "I know you're going to tell me you were always with me and Teddy, but the fact is you weren't here in the flesh. You weren't present for the parent-teacher conferences and when he had soccer practice and had to come home to do homework after-ward, even though he was bone-tired. Or for when he lost his first tooth and went to his first school dance. I know you were here in spirit, but you weren't here to help me shoulder the burden. I'm not complaining. I'm just letting you know how I feel."

Phillip was silent for a moment, which made Sophia wonder if he had disappeared, but then he spoke. "I do understand what you are saying. And I do feel for how you had to shoulder the brunt of the responsibility. I'm grateful that Cathy and Bob and your grandmother could be there to help you, but I know it was tough. I watched on many occasions as you wept at night after you put Teddy to bed. I tried to console you, and I hope I succeeded at least a little bit."

Sophia sighed. "This is the part that confuses me. From discussions with my grandmother, it's my understanding we plan with some assistance our journeys here." Sophia stopped talking as a lump formed in her throat and tears sprang to her eyes.

As she reached for a napkin to dab the tears, Phillip said, "So, the question you have—the one you've been afraid to ask yourself and me—is why didn't I love you enough to stay with you in this lifetime?"

Sophia stopped wiping her face, feeling a wave of anguish wash through her. "Yes, that is my question, Phillip. Please tell me you can answer. Because if you say it is something I'm to figure out myself at a mythical time in the future, I don't think I ever want to speak to you again."

"I am going to tell you something I haven't told you before," he said.

Sophia sat up straighter, the napkin balled in her fist. "Good, I'm listening."

"This is something you haven't thought about. It's something you urge clients to do when you are doing couples counseling, for instance, but it's something you haven't considered when it comes to us and what happened with us in this lifetime. And that is there are two people tangoing here—you and me. That means two souls meant to learn from one another. Two souls who agreed before they came back to this earth for this current lifetime to make concessions so that the other could learn valuable lessons."

As what Phillip said sank in, Sophia gasped. "Are you telling

45

me I wanted to learn certain lessons, and so you made the concession to leave me in this lifetime?"

"Yes, that is exactly what I am saying."

Sophia smacked her fist on the island. "Well, how foolish of me!"

Phillip chuckled. "There's the spark I like to see. But it was far from foolish, and you know that. As I've told you before, you planned to help many people in this lifetime. You have, you are, and you will continue to do so."

"And I never would have in such a profound and far-reaching manner if I hadn't lost you in this lifetime. Is this where I thank you for leaving me? I'm not sure I can do that."

"No need, my love. You thank me each time you help someone." And with that Phillip disappeared.

Chapter Ten

T he next morning after Sophia poured herself coffee, she called Ryan.

"Sophia, lovely to hear from you."

At the evident pleasure in his tone, Sophia felt a rush of excitement that settled somewhere in her toes. "Good morning, Ryan, I hope I'm not interrupting you from getting ready for a class."

"No, I'm all set to freak out my students with a pop quiz." He laughed.

"I used to hate it when the instructors did that, but I can understand why you must."

"Well, I know you didn't call to discuss my soon to be groaning students. What's on your mind?"

"I know we are going out on Saturday, and I'm looking forward to it. I'm calling about another invitation for us." She thought how strange it felt to refer to herself as a couple.

"Another chance to see you. If I'm free, it's a definite yes."

Sophia laughed. "You haven't heard the invitation. What if I asked you to climb Mt. Kilimanjaro?"

"I'd be up for the task. Although, while I'd love to go to Tanzania with you, I'm guessing your invitation is closer to home?"

"Tustin, to be exact. Phillip's sister, Cathy, has invited us over to dinner with her and her husband, Chuck. Besides a meal, also on the agenda is checking out Phillip's class notes." She paused to let what she said settle in.

"I have to admit I hadn't expected that," said Ryan.

"If it makes you uncomfortable, I understand."

"On the contrary, I'd love to officially meet Phillip's sister. And seeing his notes would be a blast from the past."

"Are you sure?" asked Sophia.

"I'm positive."

"How about Sunday night? There is some information I'm hoping to find in Phillip's notes that could help me with a current client, so I'd like to check them out soon."

"Two nights in a row with you, Sophia. It's a big yes, let's do it."

"Okay, wonderful. Have a great day and don't scare your students too badly."

"I can't make any promises about that. You have a wonderful day, too."

"He is crazy about you, you know," said the woman's voice she heard the night before when Sophia hung up.

"You're my life guide, aren't you?"

"I am."

"What is your name?"

"You know my name. You've seen it in your mind's eye."

"Athena."

"Exactly."

Sophia smiled, feeling like a schoolgirl with a crush. "You really think he likes me?"

Her life guide laughed then, a high-pitched tinkling sound that reminded her of the Good Witch of the West. "I know so. But enough fiddling around. Your client needs you today."

Sophia glanced at the clock. Athena was right. She didn't have much time before Gerald came in for his appointment. After putting her coffee in a travel mug, she dashed to her room to change.

A half hour later when Gerald walked into the waiting room at the counseling office, she nearly gasped at his appearance. The once put together man looked like he'd been through the spin cycle of a washing machine.

He held up his arms and dropped them to his sides. "I know. I look terrible. Don't be alarmed. It's a long story."

Sophia gestured to the coffee machine. "Would you like a cup?"

He shook his head vigorously. "No, I've had enough adrenaline over the last several hours to last a lifetime."

Sophia turned toward the hallway and said over her shoulder, "Let's get to my office and you can tell me all about it."

Once they'd gotten comfortable, she waited for Gerald to speak.

Finally, after some long moments, he said, "I was up all night with May."

Sophia hadn't expected that. She raised her eyebrows.

At the look on her face, Gerald waved his hand in the air. "Nothing like that. I'll admit there is an undeniable attraction between the two of us, but I have refused to act on it. She is a fan, and much too young for me."

"How many years younger, if I may ask?"

Gerald got a flush of pink on his complexion. "I can't believe I'm about to say this out loud. Eighteen years. It sounds so much worse when I verbalize it."

Sophia shifted in her chair. "It's not all that many years, given where you are both at in life, but I understand your reticence. Now, back to what you were doing last night."

Gerald nodded. "It was about eleven o'clock, and I was getting ready to go to bed when May called. I know I probably shouldn't have given her my personal cell number, but..." He threw up his hands. "I can't explain any of this. She has some sort of hold on me."

At the distraught look on his face, Sophia assured him, "That is perfectly normal with past life circumstances, as I've mentioned. I wouldn't be too hard on yourself. Go on."

Gerald took a deep breath and continued. "When she called, she was hysterical, telling me that her father was in danger, and they were going to kill him, and her."

Sophia sat up straighter. "That sounds ominous. Was there any truth to her claims?"

Gerald's brow furrowed. "I'm afraid so. Of course, when she called me, I wasn't sure, but I agreed to go to her apartment in Little Saigon."

Fascinating, thought Sophia. "Is she Vietnamese?"

"Her father is Vietnamese and her mother was American."

"Was?"

"She lost her to breast cancer a couple of years ago, which was when everything went south for her father, from what I can tell. May, whose given Vietnamese name is Mai, is an only child and as such became responsible for her father when her mother died—in terms of checking in on him and ensuring his wellbeing."

Sophia nodded.

"He reacted badly to the loss of his wife and began gambling. He owns a dry-cleaning business in Little Saigon he started siphoning money from to pay for his growing gambling debts."

Sophia could see where this was heading. "Is her father now in trouble with some bad people?"

Gerald nodded. "Very bad people. A group of ruthless loan sharks from a Vietnamese gang. He's into them for fifty grand."

"Oh, my. So, how does that fit in with what occurred last night?"

Gerald ran his hands through his hair. "May asked me to go help find her father, who was in the process of trying to earn the money to pay the loan sharks at an illegal card game. But he was gambling with the rest of their money, and she feared he would lose it all. The gang gave him until next week to pay up, or they're going to go after him, and her."

Sophia was unsure about what she should do with the information. A crime was obviously being committed, but it was hearsay, and she didn't know May's last name, or her father's.

"So, what happened last night?" said Sophia after they sat there for several long moments, the only sound the fountain trickling.

"I helped her find him in Little Saigon at an underground card game, and we pulled him out before he lost another twenty grand."

"Well, that's good."

"He was livid and threatened to disown May."

"That's common with addicts to threaten such things," said Sophia.

When Gerald didn't reply, she said, "I sense there is something else you're not telling me."

He sighed. "May had me take the money to safeguard it while she tries to figure out how to get the other thirty grand. She's working on securing a loan against the dry-cleaning business and all the equipment but it may not go through in time and may not be enough."

"Where is the money?" asked Sophia.

"I took it to my bank deposit box." He shook his head. "I can't believe she trusts me like this, but she does. If her father gets ahold of the money, he'll just go out again and lose it. Now she must deal with his wrath over not giving him the money. All of this really worries me."

"I know you are distraught, but at this point, the only thing you can do is try to remain calm. For the moment, May is safe, correct?"

He sighed heavily. "Yes."

"I think the best thing to do is another regression to see how what is happening with May and her father now ties into the past lifetime."

Gerald nodded wearily. "Somehow, I agree. I know I came here about my fear of snakes, but this seems to be much bigger than that."

Chapter Eleven

When Gerald arrived at the purple door and walked through it, he felt an excruciating pain in his side. He looked to see he was bleeding as a guard yelled in Vietnamese to continue walking. If he stopped, the guard would beat him again with the bamboo rod he wielded.

"*Đào*," shouted the guard for them to dig when they arrived at a clearing where other soldiers were shoveling holes in the soft, brown earth. The sky threatened to rain. Devan knew they would be expected to continue, no matter how muddy the site got. The holes they dug were meant for the severely wounded and dead. He had watched on several occasions in horror as the Viet Cong heaved men into such open graves and proceeded to bury them alive.

When the guard raised the cane, Devan fell to his knees and dug with his hands. The sky opened up then, sending rivulets of water into the holes. It was a fool's errand, he thought as they dug and the mud slipped back in as the rain pounded.

Sophia watched as Gerald made motions with his arms. A few times, he spoke in what she thought was Vietnamese. At one point, he looked as if he might cry, but then his expression became resolute once again.

When there was silence for some time, she asked, "Where are you right now?"

"I'm digging graves in Vietnam for the Viet Cong."

"Who is there?"

"Me and some other POWs."

"Is anything of significance happening, or would you like to go through another door and see what you see?"

"I want to do that."

"Find the purple door and step through it."

Devan found himself at the waterfall. He peered over the edge to see water thundering its way into a chaotic abyss. He had no more time to waste. The Viet Cong were steps away. Over the sound of the water, he heard the order to catch him. *"Bắt lấy anh ta!"*

The thought of going back to the underwater cage was much worse than what he was about to do. Just as hands reached out to grab him, Devan threw himself over the edge.

At first, he fought against the velocity of the water as it pulled him down and tossed him around. But when water entered his lungs, he felt a sense of peace. He floated now as he spotted a white light where his grandfather and grandmother and distant cousin, who had died as a child, waited for him. Overwhelmed with joy, he headed toward them, but then a terrible pain shot through his leg, and he vomited up water from his mouth and nose. He found himself lying in shallow water as a young Vietnamese woman stared down at him. "*Bạn có ổn không?*" she asked, which Devan knew meant, are you alright?

Devan's leg seized then, and he cried out in pain. The woman saw his swollen leg and her eyes widened. She grabbed him by the shoulders and dragged him along the sandy shore, shouting "*Xin Cha giúp đỡ.*"

Within a few moments, an older man came and threw Devan over his shoulder, then ran toward a small hut on the outer edge of the jungle. After setting Devan down, the man grabbed a vine and tied it tightly around his leg above the snake bite. Then he took a small blade and stuck it in the fire burning low in the makeshift kitchen and turned to Devan.

When Devan shouted, his eyes on the blade, the woman soothed, "It okay. Father remove venom." She took his hand as the older man cut into the skin on Devan's leg and squeezed out blood.

After a few moments, he said something to his daughter, who ran outside and returned with a handful of greenery in a coconut shell that the man quickly made into a poultice and applied to the wound. As he worked, he chanted, and Devan felt himself drifting off.

When Devan stopped speaking and became peaceful, Sophia checked her phone to see their session was just about up. She decided this would be a good point to bring him back.

"I'm going to guide you to the present now by counting backward from twenty. When I reach one, you will be back here in Orange in 2022."

When Gerald's eyes sprang open, he turned to her and said, "I saw her, Dr. Strand."

"Who? May?"

He nodded, then looked at the ceiling. "She saved me. She pulled me from the water after I jumped into the waterfall escaping the Viet Cong. And her father treated the snake bite."

Sophia didn't reply but let the significance of what he said settle into the room.

He sat up slowly, his expression somber. "I owe them. That's what this is all about, isn't it?"

Sophia considered her words for a moment. "I would say that is part of what is going on here. But something tells me there is more. I suggest continuing with the sessions to see what the more is, as I think it will inform what happens now."

Gerald nodded his head slowly. "What you're saying seems right. I felt like when I was under I was watching a movie, and the movie isn't done yet."

"That's a great way to think of it. I often use that analogy to explain to people what past life regression is like."

Gerald took a deep breath. "Even though it was odd to see myself in that past lifetime, and looking for May's father last night was pretty rough, somehow I feel better. Does that make any sense? Or am I just delirious from being tired?"

"It makes perfect sense. Like I mentioned when we began treatment, as we peel away the layers by exposing the various past lifetime connections with the now, explanations and enlightenment come forth, as does healing. I'm glad you're open to continuing."

Just as she said this, Sophia saw a young woman materialize

next to Gerald. She had long, flowing black hair and wore a tender expression on her face as she patted his cheek. While the sight of her surprised Sophia, what gave her pause was the intense feeling of love emanating from the woman. Sophia wondered; did Gerald have the same feelings for her?

Chapter Twelve

"**M**om, I'm not sure what to do about Cerise," said Teddy that night over dinner. Sophia had made spaghetti, and for the first time in days, he decided to stay home and eat with her.

"What do you mean?" she asked, setting down her fork and meeting her son's gaze across the kitchen table.

Teddy sighed and ran a hand through his thick, blond hair. "She's so..." He looked down at his meal, then back up at Sophia. "I'm not sure how to explain it. It's like she's half herself."

"Cerise is in mourning right now. It will ease off in time, and she'll make her way back to herself. The best thing you can do is what you're doing. Continue to be her sounding board. Just listen."

Teddy's brow furrowed. "You say she's mourning, but no one died. She's the one who got hit by a car, not her dad, although he's the one who deserved it." Her son frowned. "I'm sorry, that was a mean thing to say. I just hate the way her father's cheating is affecting her."

"I understand, and it's very unfortunate. While Cerise isn't mourning someone who died, she is mourning something that died, and that is her parent's marriage as she once knew it and her belief in her father's faithfulness."

Teddy's eyebrows raised. "I see what you mean. That is the worst part for her—what she keeps talking about—that she can't believe her parent's marriage was a lie and that her father is a cheater."

Sophia sighed. "That all or nothing thinking is common when someone mourns. She is currently disillusioned. Her parent's marriage wasn't a complete lie, but Cerise will have to come to that realization on her own. I know you want to help her move on so she can get back to the girl you met, but it's going to take time."

Teddy nodded. "I remember learning about the stages of grief in my psychology class last year. So, you're saying she has to move through the stages?"

Sophia took a sip of water and set down the glass. "Yes, exactly. And as you may remember, one of the stages of grief is anger. It sounds like she is in that stage right now. Some people stay there for some time."

Teddy swallowed a bite of spaghetti. "It also doesn't help that her mom is still reeling from the whole thing, and that Cerise refuses to talk to her dad."

Sophia reached for a napkin. "All the more reason she needs you right now. It'll be fine, honey, I promise. Cerise is a great girl. She'll make her way through this, and she'll be the better for it in the end."

Teddy's expression became contemplative. "Is that what happened with you? Did losing my father get you to a better place?"

At the look of surprise on Sophia's face, Teddy backpedaled. "I'm sorry. I probably shouldn't have said anything. This really isn't the same thing."

Sophia shook her head. "It's okay, and it really is the same thing. I had to mourn your father, and to be honest, I still mourn him at times as we move through the various life stages we do—

like your upcoming graduation from high school and then on to college. But to answer your question, yes, in the end, I was better for it, in terms of me being able to help people who have had losses, because I've been there."

"I get that," said Teddy. "It's hard to empathize if you haven't been there."

Sophia smiled. "Exactly. You know about loss when it comes to parents, because of your father. In Cerise's case, she hasn't lost her father in the physical sense."

Teddy's eyes lit up. "That's a really good way to look at it. Thanks, Mom."

"You're very welcome. Now let's finish up dinner so we can have dessert."

Teddy laughed. "I knew you'd be happy I bought those eclairs."

The next morning, Sophia's phone rang. She checked the screen and smiled. Ryan.

"Good morning," she answered.

"Good morning to you, too. I hope I'm not interrupting anything."

"Not at all. I'm just making my morning coffee." She waited a moment, and when he didn't say anything, asked, "Is everything okay?"

Ryan cleared his throat. Was he rethinking going through Phillip's notes?

"There is something occurring for me right now that may interrupt our plans this coming weekend," he said finally.

Sophia leaned against the counter. "Okay, thank you for letting me know."

"It's my mother. She's not well."

"Oh, no, I'm sorry to hear that."

"I may need to go to Wisconsin to see her."

"Of course, don't give this weekend another thought."

"They're doing some tests at the hospital. It could all be nothing, but..." He stopped.

"But you're sensing something more?"

Ryan sighed. "Yes, the last time I visited at Christmastime; she just didn't seem herself."

"It is really difficult when your parent is not well, and then there are the miles between you," said Sophia.

"I'm sorry for laying this on you. I'm sure you hear more than your fair share of stories like this."

"No need to apologize. I'm always happy to listen," she said.

"Thank you. I'll let you know as soon as I know anything. Now, let's talk about something else. How is your day shaping up? Lots of clients?"

Sophia smiled, thinking how nice it was to have a man asking about her day. "I do have several clients, and I'm also having lunch with Cathy. A working lunch, but it's still nice to get out of the center for awhile."

"Where are you planning on going?"

"The Citrus City Grille tends to be our go-to for lunches."

"Well, have a wonderful meal and sessions with your clients."

After wishing Ryan a good day in the classroom, they hung up. Just as they did so, she saw a brief flash of him standing next to the woman she'd seen in her dream the other night at the ball.

Thirty minutes later, Sophia greeted Gerald as he walked into the counseling office. He looked more refreshed.

"Did you get a better night's sleep last night?"

"I did. Fortunately, an uneventful night as far as May and her father are concerned."

"I'm glad to hear that," said Sophia as they made their way to her office.

When Gerald had sat down and made himself comfortable, she asked, "Any epiphanies since the session yesterday?"

He folded his hands in his lap. "As a matter of fact, yes. This came to me last night when I was drifting off to sleep." He looked at Sophia, a blush crossing his face. "I'm not sure if it's relevant, but I feel the need to tell you this."

"If you are feeling compelled to tell me, then it is likely something important I should hear."

Gerald took a deep breath. "It came to me as a vision, what I'm about to tell you. So, I'm not even sure if any of this is valid."

Sophia waited.

"I saw May and me. It wasn't present day, and I don't think it was the lifetime in Vietnam. I think we lived on a farm."

Sophia waited for him to go on. When he didn't, she asked, "Anything else you saw in that lifetime that seems significant?"

Gerald looked uncomfortable. "May was holding a baby boy. I think he was my son."

Chapter Thirteen

Gerald's pronouncement hung in the air for a moment, then Sophia spoke. "Well, that is an interesting turn of events that indicates what we have been suspecting. You and May have had many lifetimes together, including as parents."

"It is looking like we are very intertwined," he agreed.

"Are you ready to do a regression and continue to put all the pieces together?" asked Sophia.

In answer, Gerald lay back on the couch and closed his eyes.

A few minutes later, when it was time for Gerald to open the purple door, he felt trepidation. So much that he considered turning around and going back. "I'm afraid to open the door."

"Why, do you know?" asked Sophia.

"I'm afraid it's going to hurt to go in there."

"Would you rather not?"

He shook his head slightly. "No, I need to go in."

When Devan walked through the door, he found himself lying in a warm, dry bed of straw. He looked up at a bamboo ceiling where faint rays of light filtered in. The trill of insects and birdsong drifted in from the jungle outside.

Just then, a young woman with long, flowing black hair ducked into the hut and came to kneel beside him.

"I know you," he said, looking into familiar brown eyes.

"You awake. Leg better," she said in answer.

As Devan looked at his leg, bandaged at the thigh, memories rushed to him of jumping into the waterfall and the woman pulling him to safety, then the man carrying him to the hut and treating his snake bite.

She picked up a coconut husk from a nearby makeshift table. "You drink." Then she gently brought the husk to his lips, and he sipped, the tepid coconut water soothing his dry lips and throat. When he finished, he lay his head back and said, "Thank you."

She put a hand on his bare arm, her touch soothing. "You sleep."

For what? He felt like asking. To live another day to perish in this humid, mosquito-infested hell hole? He felt waves of fatigue overtake him then, and he drifted off.

Moments passed and Devan found himself at a gray door. He reached out to touch the handle and felt it pulsate in his hand. As he turned the knob and pushed the door open, he was sucked through a vortex and thrown into the center of a room thrumming with loud music, red and blue strobe lights ricocheting off the walls and ceiling. He was Brock now, and this was a bad trip. He felt searing pain in his right thigh, as if he'd been stabbed multiple times. He looked down at his leg to see a snake wrapped around it, its fangs dripping with his blood. Terror lodged itself in his windpipe, and he struggled to cry out.

"It's okay, man," said the girl, who had put the tab of acid in his mouth. She held his arms down with her small, cold hands. "You're on a heavy trip. Just ride it and stay mellow."

The idea of letting the trip take over terrified Brock. He might not make it out alive.

"You're cool, you dig," the girl said, now putting a paper cup of something to his lips. "It's Tang. You'll be like the astronauts."

Brock took a drink, the taste of orange filling his senses, sending him down another spiral that felt like the floor might swallow him up. And then he saw the snake hovering above him, ready to pounce.

The girl looked up at the creature. "Far out. The viper is all about making you whole. You need it. You dig?"

When she said this, the snake pounced.

When Gerald began crying out and sheltering his face with his hands, Sophia decided to bring him back.

"I want you to return to the present," she said in a firm voice. "I'm going to count backward from ten. When you pass through the purple door, you will be back here in Orange in 2022."

Gerald's breathing had become shallow now. "Ten, nine, eight, seven. Take a deep breath and keep walking. Six, five, four, three, two, one. Open the door and step back into the now."

Sophia waited while Gerald came to. He opened his eyes slowly and turned to face her. "I was Brock again."

"I gathered that. You became very distressed. What was happening?"

"I was on an acid trip with some woman. She was trying to calm me down, but there was a snake, and it was about to bite me. She said something about it."

"What was that?"

"That I needed it, and it would make me whole."

Sophia tried to make sense of what Gerald was saying. Could it be that his lifetime in Vietnam was nothing more than an LSD trip? But that didn't feel right.

"You look as mystified as I feel." Gerald had sat up and was running his hands through his hair.

"I have to admit it's a bit confusing seeing you in these parallel lifetimes," she said. "What else happened when you were under?"

"Before the acid trip I was in May and her father's hut after I had been bitten by the snake and they pulled me from the water. She was nursing me back to health." Gerald became thoughtful. "It was calm and peaceful with May, and my leg was better. I was still run-down but on the mend. I wonder what became of me. Certainly, it was a dangerous thing for May and her father to harbor me."

Sophia shut off the recording on her phone. "That is something we will hopefully find out with your next regression. Would you like tomorrow again, same time? It's open."

Gerald nodded and stood. "Thank you, Dr. Strand. Even though what I'm seeing in the regressions can be disturbing, I somehow feel calmer after each session."

"I'm glad to hear you are feeling better. I'm going to think on this a bit more, but it seems to me the snake is symbolic in some way for you."

Gerald raised his eyebrows. "Given the fact that I haven't had an incident in this lifetime with a snake biting me, I've always wondered if that was the case. So, you're thinking if I can understand the symbolism, then I can get rid of the fear?" he asked hopefully.

"I think that is a possibility."

Gerald took his cellphone out of his pocket and powered it

on. "I've got a seminar next week with one-thousand or so atten-dees. The topic is overcoming fears and obstacles. It'd be great to have this under control by then." His phone pinged several times and his eyes flew open when he checked the screen. "Oh, no."

"A problem?" asked Sophia.

"May's father has been missing since yesterday. Excuse me, but I need to go."

"Of course," said Sophia, who watched Gerald rush down the hallway. At the sound of the front door opening and closing, an unsettled feeling swept through her, and she shivered.

Chapter Fourteen

When Sophia and Cathy sat down for lunch at Citrus City Grille a couple of hours later, she noted how tense her colleague appeared.

"You seem anxious. What's up?"

Cathy sighed. "I was going to wait until we ordered, but since you asked, we didn't get the contract renewed with the insurance company."

"What does that mean?"

"It means we may have to turn down some clients, unless they can pay cash." Cathy scowled at the menu she grasped in her hands. "I'm really concerned we're going to lose clients. Some of whom have been with us for a while."

"I'm sure there is a solution. Don't they usually have an appeal for these things?"

Cathy put down the menu, looking over Sophia's shoulder to the traffic plaza. "To be honest, I'm tired of fighting the insurance companies for every last scrap."

A waiter approached with a carafe of water and filled their glasses. "I'll be right back to take your orders," he said.

Cathy nodded absently as he made his way to the next table.

"I'm not sure what you're trying to tell me. Are you thinking of getting out?" asked Sophia.

Cathy shook her head. "No, not that drastic. I just..." She stopped talking again.

"You're tired of the insurance rigamarole. I get it. How about if we hired someone to take care of some of the grunt work. I know it wouldn't solve the problem of not getting our contract renewed. That's something you and I can look into together. But if you can get more time with clients and less time with paperwork, that might help."

Cathy took a sip of water. "I don't think we can afford to pay anyone right now."

"What about an intern? Someone with attention to detail. A student. We could pay a stipend."

Cathy's eyes brightened. "That's not a bad idea. Do you have anyone in mind?"

"Yes, Cerise."

"Teddy's girlfriend?"

Sophia nodded. "Before her accident, she told me she's thinking about majoring in psychology in college. This would give her a chance to see what the field is like. I'm thinking not right away, but maybe in the spring."

Cathy put her arms on the edge of the table. "You know, that isn't a bad idea. She seems to be a very bright girl, and we already know she has excellent judgment since she's dating Teddy. It would also be nice to have someone in the office we can trust."

Sophia smiled. "I'll bring it up the next time I see her. Now regarding the problem of the insurance rejecting us. What are you thinking?"

The waiter approached then for their order, and they both asked for salmon pasta and a Greek salad.

Once he left, Cathy crossed her arms and sat back in her chair. "I know of some practices that just work on an all-cash basis. They lose some clients, but they gain time and resources by not messing around with all the insurance paperwork. I'm not sure if I want to go that route completely or at all, but it's an option. We can also repeal the insurance company's decision, but we both know it'll be a long, uphill battle. Either way, we're going to have clients without insurance coverage."

Sophia nodded and waited for Cathy to go on.

"This is where you come in," she said then.

"Me?"

"With the past life regression therapy. We both know there is no way insurance will cover the treatment, so it's already all-cash. I'm thinking we start taking on more past life clients."

At Cathy's pronouncement, Sophia was taken aback. "I never thought I'd hear you say that."

Cathy took a sip of water. "I didn't think I'd ever say it, but since I've done the regressions with you, I've seen how helpful the modality can be, and more importantly, how it can help when other treatment methods can't."

"I hear what you're saying but I'm pretty inundated at the moment with my traditional and past life clients. I don't know that I could do much more."

"I was thinking maybe I could take on more of the traditional clients to free you up for the past life ones, and you can also teach me the technique."

Sophia sat back, stunned. "You want to learn?"

"I know I'm not as talented as you are with all of this, or your grandmother, but I'm open to learning. What do you think?"

Sophia leaned out of the way when the waiter arrived with their plates and set them in front of them. When he'd left, she said, "I'll have to give this some thought. I don't think it would be something we could do right away. You'd need quite a bit of training."

"Of course," said Cathy, who picked up a fork. "I figured as much. And it's just a thought. Maybe it won't work, but I wanted to throw it out there."

Sophia was about to take a bite of her meal when she heard

Athena's voice in her ear. "It's time to do another regression with Cathy."

"You know, I think it would be a good idea if we continued with your regressions about that past lifetime during the Great Depression. I think it might shed some light on what is going on for you now in the business."

Cathy finished chewing and swallowed. "Oh, great, so I can see what a big failure I became. I don't know about that."

"We don't know that is the case. And as you just said, the treatment modality does help. If nothing else, it will give you more experience with it."

Cathy took a sip of water and set down the glass. "You've got a good point. How about tonight? Are you free? Or do you have a date with your professor?"

"Tonight works well. Teddy is going to see Cerise, and Ryan is dealing with a personal matter. His mother isn't well. In fact, we may need to postpone Sunday."

"I'm sorry to hear that. I'm dying to meet him, but I'll just have to curb my enthusiasm." She smiled at Sophia. "I can tell by the look on your face that you really like him. I'm glad."

Sophia felt her face flush slightly. It felt odd discussing this with Cathy. "I do really like him, and I'm excited to see how things go."

"Do you have prior lifetimes with him?" she asked, seemingly out of the blue, which took Sophia off guard.

"As a matter of fact, we do. I've been trying to untangle them."

"And of course you have past lifetimes with my brother. I'd love to hear about some of them."

Sophia smiled. "I think I like this."

"What?"

"Your newfound understanding and interest in all of this. Something tells me pursuing more past life clients at the center is a good idea."

Cathy picked up her water glass. "I think that deserves a toast."

Chapter Fifteen

That evening when they had both finished up with clients, Cathy knocked on Sophia's door. "You ready for me?"

Sophia set down the client notes she'd been making and called out, "I'm good to get started on your regression, if you are."

Cathy opened the door and entered. "I locked the front door so we won't be disturbed."

"Perfect," said Sophia, who gestured to the couch. "Make yourself comfortable."

As Cathy lay down on the couch, she commented, "Hopefully, I don't fall asleep. I didn't get much shuteye last night after the news about the insurance snafu."

"Like I always tell my clients, being tired can be a good thing, because it allows me to put you under more quickly, and you tend to be more susceptible to the regression—meaning slipping into past lifetimes."

"Noted. Good information for me to have," said Cathy.

As Sophia started the meditation, she wondered. Would it be possible to train Cathy to do the past life method?

When Sophia got Cathy to the purple door a few minutes later, her sister-in-law began breathing heavily.

"Are you at the purple door?" she asked her.

"Yes."

"Are you ready to walk through it?"

Cathy put her hand to her chest. "I don't know if I can do it."

"What's keeping you from opening it?"

"I'm afraid of what I'm going to see. That it might ruin me. Ruin us."

"Us?"

"Me and Bradford."

"This is a reminder that your lifetime as Isabella is over. We are just going to see what happened so that it will inform this lifetime. You will be fine," said Sophia.

Cathy nodded, and her breathing slowed. "Okay, I know you're right. I'm going to go in now."

Isabella stepped through the doorway into their one-bedroom apartment and felt like crying as she always did when she came home from a long night at work. She knew Bradford didn't want to hear again how she wished she had listened to her instincts and not expanded the business prior to the crash, but she couldn't help thinking about it.

"I'm home," she said, forcing a smile as she walked through the door.

"How was work?"

"It was fine," she said brightly of her job at the toll road. "Of course, just about everyone who came through tonight complained about having to pay." Isabella sat down at the kitchen table to rest her tired feet.

"It's a wonderful thing that Roosevelt came up with the toll roads as a way to give people employment," said Bradford, who opened the refrigerator and took out a plate and set it in front of her.

Isabella looked at the sandwich on white bread. "Tuna again?"

"This time it's a treat. Chicken," said Bradford.

Isabella's stomach rumbled as she picked up the sandwich. "How did you manage that?"

"I sold some scraps off the Benz. That should hold us for another couple of months in terms of food and heating. We have hot water now."

At the thought of a hot bath, Isabella nearly moaned. "Thank you, Bradford. I know the Benz is your favorite, and there's not much left of it now. I also know I complain, but I'm glad we're still..." She stopped talking as she took a big bite of the sandwich.

"I'm hoping you were going to say together," he said, his eyes pleading with her like they usually did to forgive him for losing their money.

Isabella swallowed and licked her lips. "That's exactly what I was going to say."

Bradford reached over and took her hand. "We'll get through this, Izzie, you'll see. We'll be back on top one day. Let me get you some water." He got up and filled a glass at the tap, then set it down in front of her.

After she took a long drink, Isabella wiped her mouth and replied, "I used to not believe that, but lately, I'm not sure why, I feel like you're right. Maybe getting this job gave me hope. And then Bethany has her job at the grocer. Did she say when she would be home?"

"She should be home any minute. I've got a sandwich for her, too."

"You'll find something soon," said Isabella. "I know it."

Bradford sat down across from her and sighed. "I hope so.

Then maybe we can get a bigger place and Bethany won't have to sleep on the sofa anymore. Have you noticed she has been acting strange?"

Isabella finished swallowing the last of her sandwich, her stomach not yet satisfied. "What do you mean?"

He ran his hand along the table, a gorgeous piece of hand-crafted maple they had managed to save from their Park Avenue apartment. "She seems unusually distant."

Isabella considered his words. "You're right. She has been more reserved. What do you make of it?"

He shook his head, his expression concerned. "I'm not sure. I was hoping you could try to talk to her."

Isabella reached down to slip off her shoes. "I will give it a try, but you know how she has been since she was a child. So stubborn."

Bradford picked up her plate to bring it to the sink when the door opened and in stepped Bethany, her face tear streaked.

Isabella stood up quickly. "Bethany, what's wrong?"

Her daughter's face crumpled and tears flowed in earnest now.

Isabella went to her and put her hands on her shoulders. "What on earth is the matter? Did you lose your job?"

At that, her daughter began sobbing hard. Isabella took her in her arms as Bradford closed the door to the apartment to stop the neighbors from gawking.

"It's okay," she soothed. "We'll be okay."

Bethany pulled back then, her face mottled with red. "I won't be able to keep the job for long." She looked to her father, then back to Isabella. "I'm pregnant," she choked out.

When Cathy became agitated and shouted, "You're what!" Sophia decided it would be a good idea to bring her back.

"It's time to come back to the now," she said firmly. "I'm going to count back from ten, and when I reach one, you are going to step back through the purple door. Ten, nine, eight, seven. You are almost there. Six, five, four, three, two, one. Open the door and step back into Orange, January 2022."

When Cathy's eyes flew open, she bolted up on the sofa and exclaimed, "In that lifetime, Madeline got pregnant out of wedlock and had to quit her job. Talk about terrible timing. We were barely getting by as it was. Do you think seeing that is an indication that something is going to happen to derail her in this lifetime? She finally has her own dental practice up and running well." Cathy was still visibly distraught and her breathing was shallow.

"Cathy, listen to me. Just because you saw that doesn't mean Madeline will have problems in this lifetime at this point."

Cathy shook her head as if to clear it, the fog lifting from her eyes. She nodded slowly. "Okay, I hear you, and of course, you're right. I'm sorry, I don't know what came over me."

Sophia stood. "Let me get you some water. I'll be right back."

When she returned with a cup of water and handed it to Cathy, her sister-in-law took a long drink, then set the cup down on the table beside her. "It all just seemed so real. It's wild how these past life regressions are like that."

Sophia sat back down. "It is fascinating, that's for sure. Tell me what else happened. I have on the recording much of what you said, but it appeared you were speaking with someone. Was it your husband back then, Bradford?"

"You mean AKA Chuck? We were living in this depressing one-bedroom apartment. I had a job working at the tollbooth and Bradford couldn't find work, so he became Mr. Mom and made me sandwiches for dinner. Bethany's job that she was about to lose was at the local grocer stocking shelves. Chuck kept selling off pieces of the cars we bought during our heyday so we could eat and heat the apartment."

"How did you feel about seeing all of that?" asked Sophia.

"Upset, of course, and resentful. I was upset I hadn't followed my instincts and saved our money rather than expanding the business."

"If you think about the current situation with the practice, do you see any parallels?"

Cathy's eyes flew open. "Yes! It's the same feeling I've been having when I think about the insurance problem and my feelings about expanding the practice. I feel stuck and angry. So, those feelings are stemming from that lifetime?" She frowned. "Now I'm being forced to expand because of the insurance problem. What should I do about it?"

"I think you need to regress again and move forward to see how you fared after the Depression."

Cathy sighed and sat back against the couch. "I can't imagine we fared all that well, given how far we fell and how the Great Depression destroyed lives, some permanently."

Sophia didn't say anything but instead let the silence fall around them.

Finally, Cathy said, "You're right. I need to see what happened —if even to see that we lived in that apartment until our dying days. I'm guessing you're going to tell me it would be best if I waited a day or two?"

Sophia nodded. "Yes, that would be my suggestion."

"Okay, thank you for taking the time to do this. I know you had a long day, and I can tell these sessions take it out of you. They sure take it out of me. Something else for me to think about. I better get home. Chuck will be wondering where I am. You want to come over for dinner? At least it won't be a sandwich." She laughed.

"No, but thanks for the invitation. I'm going to call my grandmother. She should just be getting up."

"I'm so glad you have her wise counsel," said Cathy as they both stood.

The two women embraced, and as they did so, Sophia heard Phillip's voice in her ear, "Group hug."

Chapter Sixteen

Sophia sat in the quiet of her office at her desk as Cathy left the center. She heard her lock the front door, then the sound of her car leaving the parking lot. She picked up her cellphone and checked the time. Her grandmother would likely just have gotten up and be sitting on her patio overlooking the sea, the gulls demanding she feed them.

"Little love, I was just thinking about you. You have many questions. I can hear pandemonium inside of your head."

Sophia laughed. "Well, you are hearing right, as usual. I hope it wasn't too loud this early in the morning for you."

Her grandmother chuckled. "I can handle it, and it's not much different than usual."

Sophia sat back in her chair. "How is it Grandmother? I've wondered about that. Hearing all the voices of those trying to talk to you and all of the messages."

"You know, Sophia."

"I don't know that I know exactly."

"But you have an idea, now don't you? You often hear from Phillip, and I imagine now that you have connected with your life guide, you also hear from her."

Sophia picked up a pencil and began doodling on a notepad. "You're right, as usual."

"What you really meant to ask me is how I keep my sanity hearing all of the voices, now didn't you?"

Sophia let out a breath she didn't know she'd been holding. "You have such a way of saying what's on my mind, Grandmother. Yes, I suppose that is my question."

"You keep the faith that what you are hearing and your resulting actions are helping people. Sometimes many people, if the message reverberates. By that I mean when you help someone and then what you help them with helps many others. You've seen that with the work."

"I have seen that. I take it you're telling me, then, that the pandemonium is worth it if you're able to help people?" asked Sophia.

"That is exactly what I am telling you. Now what are your burning questions?"

"Back to my current client and the odd parallel lifetime that keeps coming up. I must admit I am stymied by this and have no idea how to translate any of it. I fear if I don't come to understand it, I won't be able to help him."

"First of all, you need to banish all doubts, Sophia. It is important at this juncture that you stop doubting your abilities in the past life work. I assure you that you have done this work before."

"I have?" said Sophia, surprised at her grandmother's words.

"Yes, you most certainly have in prior lifetimes. Now that we have that out of the way, I want you to promise me to start believing in your abilities surrounding the work. That's not to say you can't ask me questions. I welcome them, and it is a good idea, given my many years of experience. However, it's time to step up to the plate, so to speak."

Sophia sighed. "Are you telling me to put on my big girl panties?"

Her grandmother laughed. "Yes, that's exactly what I'm

telling you. You can do this, Sophia. No more doubts, okay? Questions are fine, but it is past time to stop doubting."

Sophia sat up straighter. "Understood. I have my marching orders. Can I ask my questions now?"

"You most certainly can," said her grandmother over the sound of gulls squawking.

"The last regression with my client, who will be coming in again tomorrow morning, included both lifetimes again. I'm trying to decipher what that means."

"I can see why you would have questions and some confusion. The parallel lifetimes are quite interesting, yet what do they mean? Generally, the lives that come forth are parallel in their realities, if that makes sense. Your challenge is to identify the parallels and then determine how those inherent parallels inform the current lifetime."

Sophia thought about Gerald's case. "In this case, in one of his past lifetimes he went to serve his country without question, while the other half of him became a deserter," said Sophia.

"A very powerful contrast," said her grandmother.

"But how do I untangle things and suss out the meaning from that? Any suggestions?"

"You need more information."

"So, more regressions?" asked Sophia.

"Yes, but you also know a great deal already. When you put the client under tomorrow, keep the contrast top of mind. You will likely have epiphanies along the way, as will your client. I'll be happy to revisit once that occurs. You know that."

"I do. Thank you so much."

"It's past eight there. No dinner with Teddy tonight? Or your professor?"

Sophia was about to protest at her grandmother's reference to Ryan being her professor but the sound of it pleased her, and she let it slide. "No, just me, myself, and I tonight. I think I'll pick up a pizza and go home and watch a good movie."

"That sounds delightful. I know the days doing past life regression can be long, and it's nice to have some downtime."

"Speaking of downtime, have you and Randall planned your cruise over spring break?" asked Sophia.

"Plans are in the works," said her grandmother airily.

Sophia smiled. "I'm so glad to hear that."

"Any other questions for me before we hang up so you can get to your pizza? Perhaps about you and your professor?"

Sophia flashed to her vision of the woman with Ryan she had seen in her dream. "Yes. I told you about the dream I had of me and Ryan at a ball. Well, the woman I saw standing in the shadows glaring at us I saw in my mind's eye with Ryan, but it looked like this lifetime."

"That's not surprising. We generally won't see such visions unless there is something to visit in this lifetime. Has he said anything about other women?"

"No, we haven't gotten that far in terms of getting to know one another."

"The only way to find out will be to continue to get to know one another. Do you have plans together in the near future?"

"We do, but his mother is ill, so he may be going back to Wisconsin to see her, which means our visits will have to wait. I'm not complaining. Just giving you the information."

"All in the right time," said her grandmother. "You'll see."

Sophia nodded to herself. "Yes, that I always do see. Thank you so much. I love you," said Sophia before hanging up.

"I love you more," said her grandmother.

Just as Sophia set her cellphone down, she felt a presence.

"I've had parallel lifetimes, as have you," said Phillip.

"When was that?" said Sophia, her interest piqued. "You better not tell me in this lifetime and that I could have sought you out."

Phillip laughed. "No, not in this lifetime. Our saga has kept me much too busy."

"What can you tell me about Gerald and his dual lifetimes?"

"His fear of snakes."

Sophia was surprised at Phillip's comment.

"What about his fear of snakes?"

"That is the connection here."

"How on earth is a fear of snakes a connection? I'm not seeing that."

"Take a closer look and you will."

At that, Phillip left.

Sophia gathered her things to go home. As she was leaving the office, she remembered something from Gerald's last regression. Brock had experienced the snake during his LSD trip. It appeared that Phillip might be onto something.

Chapter Seventeen

Thunder rumbled, then rain began pounding the earth, splattering mud onto Pearl's dress. She shielded her eyes from the downpour, now stinging her face. As she struggled to sit up, pain seared the back of her head, causing her to lie back down. She looked around to see she was in a hole in the earth, puddles quickly forming around her, the air thick with the smell of wet earth.

How did she end up here, she struggled to remember. She and Clifton were at the ball, and she had needed fresh air, so she went out into the estate's garden. He had warned her it would soon rain, but she assured him she would be right back.

Then what happened?

As lightning lit up the sky above, Pearl saw Gwendoline standing illuminated in the electric light. Pearl reached up her arm and cried for help but all the woman did was give her an acrid smile. And then, to Pearl's horror, she began shoveling earth into the hole.

Sophia woke with a start, her heart pounding so hard in her chest she clamped both hands on her breast to still it. As she gulped air for a few moments, she struggled to make sense of the visions from her dream. She glanced around to see she had fallen asleep on the couch. Sitting up, she reached over and picked up the glass of water on the coffee table and took several gulps, willing herself to calm down. Then she looked at the clock on the wall, which in the dim light read 3:33.

She sat there for some time, grasping at the visions from her dream, struggling to piece them together. She had been hurt, her head aching. And she had been out in a storm. She saw herself lying in the mud in a hole and heard thunder. Putting her head in her hands, she willed herself to remember what else had happened. After what seemed like an eternity with nothing coming up but a blank screen in her head, she got up and went down the hallway to her bedroom where she left her door open.

She was just getting into bed when lightning lit up the sky outside and a few moments later, the sky rumbled and raindrops began pelting the condo's roof. As this happened, she saw a vision in her head and gasped. The woman standing at the edge of the hole in her dream about to bury her alive was the same woman she'd seen at the ball and standing next to Ryan in this lifetime. She shivered and burrowed herself deep under her blankets, lying there awake for some time before finally feeling calm enough to drift off to sleep.

When Sophia awoke in the morning, rain continued to come

down. She got out of bed and looked out at the wet day, noting the stoplight on the corner was out.

She put on her robe and slippers and went into the kitchen to find Teddy wolfing down cereal.

"Morning, honey, in a hurry to get to school? You have the, 'I've got an exam look,'" she said as she opened the cupboard and pulled out a coffee mug.

Teddy swallowed a mouthful, then took a gulp of coffee. "Yep, another trig exam. I swear, this professor is a beast."

Sophia poured herself a cup of coffee. "I'd thank him, if I were you. He's getting you ready for college. Most university professors tend to be beasts."

"Great," Teddy groaned. "So, I can expect a whole lot more of this?"

Sophia laughed as she poured half-and-half into her coffee. "I'm afraid so."

"Was dad a beast when it came to his classes?"

"I'm not exactly sure. I only had him for a day." Sophia took a sip of coffee.

Teddy grinned. "Why only a day? You couldn't take the heat?"

"It turns out your father couldn't teach the class because of being in the National Guard. It was a Friday class, and he often had to do training over the weekends. But he was there for that one day. If it wasn't for that class, I don't know that we would have met."

Teddy picked up his backpack. "That's cool to think your meeting was destiny. Like me and Cerise. The fact that she transferred here her senior year. That doesn't usually happen."

Sophia walked over to her son and ran her fingers through his blond mop, pushing his bangs out of his eyes. "I guarantee you that your and Cerise's meeting was destined. Just like mine and your father's."

Teddy cocked his head to one side. "So, you're saying I was always supposed to meet Cerise? That it was my fate?"

"That's exactly what I'm saying."

"I like that." Then he gave her a quick hug and called over his shoulder as he strode out of the condo, "Love you!"

"I love you exponentially more," she called after him.

"There isn't much that love can't cure," said Phillip then.

Sophia, who was about to go to her room to dress for work, stopped. "What does that mean, exactly? I feel like you're trying to tell me something."

"I am, in a way. I'm not able to share the future, as is often the case, but I assure you love does conquer all."

"Are you referring to me and Ryan and the terrible nightmare I had last night?"

Silence.

"Phillip?"

But he was gone.

Chapter Eighteen

"I hate to say this, but you look worse than I've ever seen you," said Sophia later that morning as Gerald settled on the couch for his session. He appeared to have hastily dressed in jeans and a T-shirt, and his beard looked like it needed trimming. His hair and clothing were damp, which told her he hadn't bothered with an umbrella.

Gerald sighed. "You are definitely seeing me at my worst. Actually, I'm seeing me at my worst. I have no idea what has become of my life. It's as if it has unraveled right before my eyes. How am I going to do my seminar in a few days?"

Sophia felt badly for her part in what was occurring, but then reminded herself the past life regression therapy was often messy.

"Why don't you tell me what happened. I'm sensing something with May?"

Gerald slumped back on the couch. "I was with her all night. Her father is officially missing, and she is a wreck."

"Does it have anything to do with the gambling debt?"

He ran his hand over his beard, as if doing so could tame it. "We're thinking most likely. The debt isn't due yet, so he is probably at an underground card game, but we checked every one we could find last night." Gerald frowned. "I don't have a good feeling about this."

Sophia felt a sense of foreboding, as well. Rather than mentioning it, she said, "Well, I'm glad you made it here to your appointment. The sooner we get to the bottom of what happened in that lifetime in Vietnam, the sooner I think you'll have some answers about May and her father's situation."

Gerald let out a long breath. "And hopefully we'll shed some light on what's going on between May and I, too."

"Did something happen between you two last night? Besides trying to find her father?"

Gerald sighed. "Yes. We kissed. That's as far as it went, but that's all it took. Now I've crossed a line, and I'm not sure there is any going back."

Sophia picked up her phone so she could set it to record. "You mean you both crossed a line. I'm assuming it was a mutual desire to kiss one another?"

Gerald nodded vigorously. "Of course, I would never take advantage of her or the circumstances. I'm not sure how it happened, but it just did. And I think, okay, I know, she wanted it, too."

"You obviously have a very strong connection with May. And I know her being younger concerns you. But an eighteen year difference in age, while substantial, is not uncommon. Of even more significance is the fact that you've known each other before —most likely over many lifetimes. Chronological age doesn't really count when we're talking hundreds of years."

Gerald's pensive expression relaxed at Sophia's words. "I'm going to remind myself of that."

"Great. Are you ready?"

"Definitely." Gerald laid down on the couch and closed his eyes.

Devan was back in Vietnam. This time, he stood next to a small fire cooking rice when Lan came up and tried to take the wooden spoon from him. "Me," she said.

"I'm capable of stirring some rice." Devan looked at his leg where the snake had bitten him. There was a chunk of skin missing, but the wound had healed without infection.

Lan giggled as she lunged for the spoon. "You sit."

Devan took her by surprise by grabbing her and pulling her close, then kissing her, long and deep. As she melted into his embrace, he marveled as he had over the last three months at finding such a beautiful, kind woman in what had once been hell.

When they pulled apart and she tried again to grab the spoon from his grasp, he held it aloft and ordered, "You sit."

He was about to kiss her again, when Hieu, her father, came running up, terror on his face.

"What is it father?" Lan asked.

Hieu gestured to Devan. "He hide. Viet Cong coming."

Devan knew what to do, as they had rehearsed this many times. He ran to the back of the hut and into the jungle to the spot where they had dug a hole. Then he scaled the opening as quickly as possible, and Lan and her father covered the top with bamboo fronds and left.

It wasn't long before Devan heard shouting in Vietnamese. He strained to make out what was being said, but he only caught a word here and there. At one point, he heard Hieu yell out, and then Lan screamed.

After the yelling, it became silent. Had they taken Lan and her father? Over the next few minutes, which felt like days, Devan thought he might lose his mind with worry. But then the fronds were pulled away, and he blinked into the midday sun. "Lan," he whispered loudly, relief flooding through him at seeing her face. "What happened?"

"They take bố," she cried.

"Why did they take your father?"

"They say he hide prisoner."

Devan's heart fell. So, the Viet Cong were looking for him, and they suspected Hieu and Lan. He had to give himself up to save them.

"Can you throw down the rope?" he asked.

Lan nodded and left for a few minutes, returning with a rope made of palm fronds. He grasped hold of it and pulled himself up and out. When he emerged, he assured her, "We'll get your father back."

She looked at him, her face streaked with tears. "How?"

"I'll go to them. It's me they want."

Lan shook her head vigorously, her eyes saucers of fear. "No, they kill us all."

Devan thought about what Lan said. She was right. They would kill her and her father for harboring him, and probably torture him in front of them first. As if she read his thoughts, Lan began sobbing. He held her close, feeling so helpless and angry with himself. What kind of man was he that he couldn't keep her safe?

When Gerald began murmuring and appeared distressed, Sophia asked him, "Where are you now?"

"I'm with Lan. They have her father. I don't know what to do."

"Who has her father?"

"The Viet Cong."

At the look of anguish on his face, Sophia asked, "Do you want to come back now?"

He shook his head. "No. I need to see what happened."

"How about going through another door to the future?" she said.

Gerald nodded.

"Okay, step through the purple door and tell me where you are."

It took a few minutes before Gerald spoke again. He didn't look pleased.

"What do you see now?" she asked him.

"It's not good, man. They're making me stay in this little beat-up cabin in the woods."

"Brock, is that you?"

"Yeah, it's me. Who would it be?"

"Where is the cabin?"

"In Canada out in the middle of nowhere. I can't get a job because I don't have any documents."

"Are you all alone?"

"Yeah. I'm not sure I made the right choice."

"You mean you should have stayed and gone to war?"

He wiped his hand across his brow. "I don't feel so good about this anymore. Almost all of my friends went to Nam, and here I am." He turned to face her, and she noted the pain in his eyes—much different than the free-loving Brock she'd met before. "Do you think I'm a bad person?" he asked her.

Sophia thought about her answer for a moment. "I think you were afraid about going to war, and rightfully so. You made the best decision for yourself at the time, but we all make decisions we regret."

"The worst part is I left Cheryl."

Sophia waited to see if he would say anything else, but when he remained silent, she asked, "What's happening now, Brock?"

"I think I'm always going to be alone. It's a drag, man."

"Do you want to move forward and see if you are alone in the future?"

Suddenly, Gerald's face contorted, and he yelled, "No, I don't."

Chapter Nineteen

Sophia considered for a moment what to do next. Given the fact that May's father was officially missing, she felt she needed to push Gerald to see if he could reveal more.

"Brock, I think you will feel better if you walk through the purple door."

He continued to shake his head vehemently. "I don't want to. This has all been a real drag. They're calling us cowards, and who knows what they'll do to us next. If I can't get the fake documents that say I'm Canadian, I don't know what I'm going to do."

"Why not just take a peek through the doorway to see what happened?" she suggested.

Brock stopped shaking his head and remained still for a moment.

After a few beats, she asked, "Have you taken a look through the doorway, Brock?"

"Who's Brock? Why do you keep mentioning him?"

"Apologies, is this Devan?"

"Of course."

"What's happening right now, Devan?"

"Lan and I are in bed together."

This took Sophia by surprise. "Oh, and you are being intimate?"

He nodded and frowned.

"Is the experience not a good one?"

"It was wonderful. I don't think I've ever loved anyone before. I mean, I thought I loved my fiancé back home, but with Lan, it's different."

"How so?" asked Sophia, unsure why this line of questioning was so important but she felt she needed to ask.

Devan became contemplative. "Because she accepts me completely for who I am, and because, most importantly, she doesn't want anything from me but my companionship."

"She enjoys you for you, then. Where are you both?"

"We're in the hut, and it's nighttime."

"Is her father there?"

He shook his head. "That's why I'm feeling badly about this. He's being held by the Viet Cong, and here I am..." He trailed off.

"In bed with his daughter."

His expression became anguished. "I should be trying to save her father. I know how horrible the Viet Cong can be."

"What is stopping you?"

He threw up his hands. "I'm overpowered by them. I know that. May knows that. But I don't know if I can live with myself if I don't try."

"What will you do?"

Gerald's expression became peaceful. "Lan is sleeping now. She looks happy." Then he grimaced. "I must leave her, though. I won't live with myself if I don't try to help her father."

Devan waited until Lan was fast asleep before he slid out of her arms and quietly put on his clothing. He burned with shame, knowing her father was being held, and he had just made love to his daughter. He knew what the Viet Congs did at night. They would be torturing Hieu with water and snakes, and animals they had starved, such as wild boar. It might be a suicide mission, but he had to do his best to save him.

When Sophia's phone indicated their session was ending, she said gently, "It's time to come back to the present now."

"But I'm just about to the Viet Cong encampment," Gerald said, his voice a low whisper. "They are about to change the guards. I'll have about thirty seconds to go in and grab May's father."

Sophia wasn't sure what to do. If she pulled him out, she had no way of knowing when or if he would reach this point again. But she had a client coming in for traditional therapy soon. Making a split-second decision, she said, "Okay, go ahead."

Then she texted Cathy to tell her client she'd be with her as soon as possible. When she finished, she noted that Gerald's breathing had become labored, and sweat had formed on his brow.

Devan crept toward the tent where he knew they were holding May's father, because, while waiting in the shadows for an opening, he had heard him cry out several times. When the next set of guards approached and began speaking with the guards on duty in front of the tent, he ran around to the back and slipped underneath.

He stopped himself from crying out at what he saw. May's father splayed out, a knife pinning his hand to the slab of wood on which he lay. When he saw Devan, his eyes widened.

Devan rushed to the man, grabbing the knife and pulling upward with force. As he did so, Hieu cried out, which caused a guard to come in. Devan used the knife to defend himself, plunging it into the man's stomach.

"Go!" he shouted to May's father, who had managed to stand. Within seconds, he slipped underneath the tent and hopefully to safety.

Sophia waited as long as she could, then called Gerald back. "I am going to count backward from ten and then you are going to be back here in Orange," she told him. "Ten, nine, eight. You are heading back to 2022. Seven, six, five, four. You are almost back. Three, two, one. Open your eyes. You are now in the present."

When Gerald's eyes sprang open, he said, "I saved May's father. I saw him escape. But I'm not sure I made it out alive, or what happened to May."

Sophia let what Gerald said settle in the air for a moment. "I suppose it's possible that none of you survived the situation, but we won't know for sure unless we do more regressions," she said.

He sat up and pulled his phone from his pocket and checked the time.

"I let you stay under for a while longer, because you were getting to the critical point where you left May to go attempt to rescue her father," said Sophia.

Gerald nodded as he stared at his phone. Then he looked up at Sophia, his eyes wide. "I slept with her before I went to rescue her father."

"It appears so."

"I loved her."

"That appeared to be the case, as well."

He shook his head slightly. "I never thought when I came through these doors that this would happen. All of this has taken me completely by surprise."

"That's generally what happens with the past life regression therapy. You learn and experience much more than you ever imagined possible. I know it can be overwhelming, but it does usually help clear things up as to what is occurring in this lifetime." Her phone pinged then, and she checked the screen. Cathy letting her know her next client had arrived and was waiting in the waiting room.

"It seems like May and her father and I are repeating a pattern in this lifetime. Is that common?"

"Very common."

"Does that mean my life could be in danger with all of this?" he asked.

Sophia shifted in her seat. "Given that her father is involved with very dangerous people, I would think yes."

"Maybe I should advise May to contact the authorities. And as for continuing sessions, this seems to have opened a powder keg I'm not sure I should allow to explode."

Sophia stood. "Going to the police sounds like a prudent thing to do at this point, especially since her father is missing."

Gerald faced her. "Thank you for today and for extending the time. I'm sorry to have thrown off your schedule."

"Don't worry about it. It was my call. I'm just glad you got some clarity. Although..." She stopped talking.

Gerald raised his eyebrows.

"There do seem to be a lot of loose ends here," she continued. "Including how your alternate self as Brock fared being a deserter, and have we effectively dealt with your fear of snakes?"

Gerald slid his phone into his pocket. "I'd like to think about all of this. I feel less pressure around the idea of snakes, although I don't know if that is because this whole thing with May has distracted me."

"Of course, I'm here if you need me," said Sophia.

They walked out of her office and down the hall. When they reached the waiting room and her client saw them, she exclaimed, "You're Gerald Walker. I've read all your books. My favorite was *Fear Not, Your Life Awaits.*"

Gerald may have been surprised, but he didn't show it. Instead, he extended his hand and said, "Very nice to meet you, Miss?"

"Aronson," she gushed. "Rachel Aronson. My friends are going to be so impressed I met you in person." She looked from Gerald to Sophia, her expression curious.

Sophia turned to Gerald. "Thank you so much for coming in. I value your opinion on the matter we spoke about."

Looking visibly relieved, Gerald smiled. "You're very welcome, Dr. Strand. I'm glad I could help." Then he bowed slightly to them both. "I'll let you ladies get to things. Have a great rest of the day."

Once he'd left, Rachel still gaping, Sophia suggested, "Want to get to my office so we can start your session. I apologize about starting late. If you're able to stay past the hour, we can make up the difference."

"I can, Dr. Strand," she said as she followed Sophia to her office. "I can't believe I met Mr. Walker. He's such an inspiration to so many people."

Chapter Twenty

L ater that afternoon as she packed up for the day, Sophia's phone rang. She smiled and answered. "Hi, Ryan."

"I hope I didn't catch you in the middle of work."

"I finished with my last client a bit ago, so I'm all yours."

"I like the sound of that, but I'm afraid I don't have good news. My mother's condition has deteriorated, so I'm getting on a flight tonight for Wisconsin."

"I'm so sorry to hear about your mother. Don't give our plans another thought," said Sophia.

"I've been giving our plans quite a few thoughts and was looking forward to seeing you. I'm really sorry I have to cancel."

Sophia's heart warmed at his words. "I was looking forward to getting together, too, but family comes first."

"I know this is the last minute, but would you like to take me to the airport? We could catch a quick bite on our way."

At the suggestion, Sophia found herself beaming. "That would be great. When do you need to leave?"

"If you could get to my place within the hour, that would work. I'll text you my address."

"I'll be over in the next thirty to forty minutes," said Sophia, thinking how she could go home and get freshened up. She said goodbye to Ryan, then rushed into the hallway, nearly running into Cathy.

"I'm so sorry. I should have been paying more attention."

Cathy held a coffee cup aloft and said, "No harm, no foul. I didn't spill a drop. No more clients today?"

"All done."

Cathy cocked her head. "You look excited. Where you off to?"

Sophia felt her face flush.

Cathy grinned. "A date with the professor?"

"I'm taking him to the airport. It turns out his mother is doing very poorly, so he's flying out to Wisconsin tonight."

Cathy frowned. "Oh, I'm sorry to hear that. I guess that means we won't be seeing him this Sunday?"

"Probably not. I'll be there, though. I really want to take a look at Phillip's class notes. And see you and Chuck, of course."

Cathy laughed. "Of course." Then she stepped aside. "Don't let me keep you."

As Sophia left the office, she thought how odd this seemed to be talking to Cathy about a man other than her brother. It would take some getting used to.

When she arrived home, she found Teddy in the kitchen piling cold cuts onto bread. "You're home early," he said.

She set her purse on the island and went to get a drink of water. "I'm about to leave again."

"Where are you going?" asked Teddy as he slathered mayonnaise onto his sandwich.

"Maybe it's none of your business," she said, putting her glass in the sink.

"Woah, are you meeting Professor Collins?" Teddy grinned.

"Yes, I'm taking him to the airport. His mother is unfortunately ill, so he's going home to Wisconsin. We're going to catch dinner before his flight."

"I'm sorry to hear about his mom, but I'm not sorry that you're seeing him," said Teddy, who picked up his sandwich to take a bite.

A smile tugged at Sophia's lips as she made her way down the hallway to her bedroom to get ready.

When Sophia pulled up in front of Ryan's house twenty minutes later, she was greeted by a charming Craftsman home painted in white with army green trim. Flower beds lined the front of the house and the walkway, created from slate pavers. In the middle of the small lawn was a birdbath, now brimming with rainwater.

She walked up the steps to the porch and was about to knock when the door opened.

"Right on time. Come on in for a moment while I make sure I've got everything."

Sophia stepped in as Ryan held the door open, a shiver of delight racing up her spine as it always did when she was this near to him. As if reading her thoughts, he pulled her to him and gave her a kiss that made her lips feel like they were suddenly lit on fire. When they finished, he said, "Forgive me for being so forward, but I just couldn't help myself."

Sophia smiled. "I think that was the perfect way to greet me."

"I like the sound of that," said Ryan, who stepped back so she could enter and pointed to the couch. "Have a seat."

Sophia went to sit, glancing around the inviting living room to see that Ryan had done a good job of decorating in the Craftsman period style. The couch's earthy tone complemented the room's warm color palette and oak flooring. Built-in cabinets ran along one wall, the shelving lined with books. Framed nature-inspired artwork adorned the walls, and several large plants lent warm greenery to the space. Along another wall, the fireplace took center stage. Constructed of sand-colored brick, she imagined it kept the room warm on cold nights.

Spying a couple of framed photos on the intricately carved wooden mantel, she got up and went to look at them. One photo featured several people, including a younger Ryan, standing under a sycamore, its leaves beginning to turn shades of yellow and brown. The other photo pictured an older Ryan and a boy of about six. They stood grinning into the camera in front of a lake, fishing rods in hand, the sun bright at their backs.

"I see you found the photo of me and Jake," said Ryan, who had come up behind her.

"He looks just like you. Is he related?" She turned to face him, her smile disappearing at the look on his face. "Did I say something?"

Ryan sighed. "I hadn't planned on broaching this subject yet, but I did invite you into my home, and of course, you would see the photo. That's my son."

Sophia was taken aback. "You have a son. I had no idea."

Ryan eyed the photo again, then met Sophia's eyes. "Had. He died."

Sophia gasped. "Oh, Ryan, I'm so sorry. When did he pass?"

"Ten years ago. I'm sorry to have made you uncomfortable."

Sophia moved closer. "You haven't made me uncomfortable at all. The news just took me by surprise."

Ryan looked over at his luggage. "How about we get to the airport? There's an Italian restaurant near there."

When they were settled in the car, Sophia behind the wheel driving down the street, Ryan said, "It was a terrible accident."

Sophia glanced over at Ryan, then back at the road as she got in the right lane to get on the 55 Freeway. "That must have been very painful for you, and his mother."

Her last two words hung in the air for a moment before Ryan spoke. "We never married—his mother and I."

Why had Sophia been so nosy and looked at the photo! And since they'd met, she had spoken freely of Teddy, which was something she wouldn't have done if she'd known.

"There was some question as to Jake's mother's part in his death," he said.

At his words, Sophia suddenly saw a car upturned on the side of the road. "Was it a car accident?" she asked.

"Yes, and his mother may have been drinking."

Sophia turned on her blinker and switched lanes. "I'm sorry. I really didn't mean to pry."

"You're not prying. It's something I probably should have told you from the get-go, in case..." he trailed off.

"In case what?" She looked at his profile as he stared straight ahead. "In case I felt it was best we don't get involved?"

He sighed. "Yes."

"Well, as you know, I've had my share of loss. And I'm a therapist, remember? I don't scare easily." Sophia took the turnoff to John Wayne Airport. "Which way do I go on MacArthur?"

"Right, then Antonello's is on the left."

When she parked, Sophia turned to Ryan. "This obviously isn't the ideal time to discuss this, but I'm glad you told me. I really like you, Ryan, and I want to get to know you. I'd love to hear all about Jake sometime." There, she had said what was on her mind. She waited for his response.

Ryan gave her a small smile. "I've found that when people find out about Jake, they start tiptoeing around the topic, and things often become so awkward that it's impossible for us to get to know one another."

Sophia looked out the window to see night settling in and the parking lot lights flicker on. "It's difficult for many people to process the loss of people others hold dear. It's not that they don't want to say and do something helpful or show they care. They simply just don't have the capacity."

Ryan smiled. "The more I get to know you, Sophia, the more I understand why Phillip was so crazy about you. You see the big picture, but you're not afraid to get down to the details—to what really matters." Ryan motioned to open his door. "Shall we?"

Once they had settled at a table and ordered, Ryan, obviously determined to lighten the mood, asked, "Is your grandmother still seeing Randall?"

"Yes. They're currently planning a trip together during spring break when he has time off from classes."

Ryan laughed. "This could become a very expensive relationship."

Sophia picked up a piece of bread from the basket the waiter had just set down. "I have a feeling that isn't a problem for either of them."

They spent the rest of their short meal discussing Ryan's classes and the often-amusing subjects of some of the students' term papers.

Before long, it was time to get him to the airport. When she pulled up in front of American Airlines, he turned to her. "Thanks for the enjoyable meal. I know we started out on a serious note, but the laughs over dinner helped me get ready for what is going to be a rough trip."

Sophia put her hand on his forearm. "I'm glad I could help. I had a very nice time."

Ryan leaned over and gave her a kiss. "I'll call you."

Then he got out of the car and pulled his suitcase from the back seat, turning to wave one more time as he headed into the terminal. Just as the automatic door opened, Sophia saw a young boy materialize by his side and take his hand.

Later that night after Sophia had gotten ready for bed, she took her laptop out of its case and set it on her bed and powered it on. Then she pulled up Google and did a search on Ryan's son's accident. In a way, she felt like she was invading his privacy, but something told her she needed to understand what happened.

Before long, she found a newspaper article about the tragic accident. The article featured a photo of the boy she'd seen with Ryan, and someone she hadn't expected to see. The face of the woman in her past life who had buried Sophia alive—Jake's mother.

Chapter Twenty One

Sophia awoke the next morning with the newspaper article still in her mind. From her estimation, Ryan was in his forties, like Sophia. That meant he was most likely in his twenties when his son was born.

Sophia sighed. There was so much she didn't know about the man, but at the same time, she felt like she knew him intimately. Was this how it was for her past life clients? This unsettling push and pull between the then and the now?

She thought about Gerald and his current tendency to want to run from the situation with May the more intense things became. If she was being honest with herself, though she told Ryan she didn't scare easily, the more she saw of her past lifetimes with him, the more uneasy she became.

Her phone rang then, and she checked the screen. It was Gerald.

"Dr. Strand, thank goodness you answered. I'm in need of some advice. Is this a good time?"

Sophia sat up in bed and put a pillow behind her back. "Yes, it's fine. I'm listening."

"May is..." he stopped talking for a moment, a catch in his voice.

Sophia pulled up the blind next to her bed as she waited, glimpsing the sun attempting to peek through the gray clouds that layered the sky.

"I'm sorry," he said, finally. "This experience has been so emotional for me."

"I hear you, Gerald. And I do understand. I know this is a lot. How about starting from the beginning? What has happened since you left your session yesterday?"

He let out a big breath. "I went to my office to attempt to work but I just couldn't think, even though I have many emails to answer regarding my upcoming seminar, and final details to take care of. I couldn't stop thinking about May and how she must be so scared about her father. In fact, this may sound strange, but I could *feel* her distress."

"That doesn't sound strange at all. With individuals with whom we have strong connections, we will often feel their feelings, both good and bad."

"I don't think I've ever truly been in love," Gerald said suddenly. "I thought I was, but this with May. It's just so different. So much richer and fuller and frightening than anything I've ever experienced. Ironic given that I teach people to live their best lives."

As he said this, Sophia thought about Devan and Brock and what they had said about not having experienced true love.

"Did you suggest to May she go to the police about her father?"

"Yes, and she flat out refused. She and her father don't trust them."

"The only thing I can say is that further regressions will likely shed more light on what you should do," said Sophia. "There's no guarantee, but I've found with other clients it does help, and often greatly."

"I feel what you are saying is right. Do you have time this morning?"

"I do happen to have a bit of time this morning. How about in an hour?"

"I'll see you then. Thank you so much, Dr. Strand. And I appreciate your discretion yesterday with my fan."

Forty minutes later, Sophia walked into the counseling office to find that Cathy had already brewed coffee. That would give her time to get into her office and prepare for Gerald's visit, including checking her notes from the last session.

But just as soon as she had settled at her desk, Cathy barreled in.

"They're threatening to cancel the liability insurance," she said, waving a piece of paper in the air.

"Why?" asked Sophia.

Cathy looked at the paper. "It isn't clear. Something about malfeasance in terms of conduct." She threw herself into the chair across from Sophia's desk. "We've done nothing wrong. I can't imagine what this is about."

Sophia held out her hand. "May I?"

Cathy handed the document over and tapped her foot on the floor while Sophia checked it out.

"Something tells me this is a clerical error," she said when she finished reading it.

Cathy threw up her hands. "And what makes you think that?"

Sophia didn't answer.

Cathy looked around the room. "Is this something you're being told from the other side?"

"It's a feeling I have, yes." Sophia looked at the paper again. "How about I make some calls on this later this afternoon to try to get to the bottom of things. I think you're too close to it."

Cathy put her head in her hands, nodding as she did so. "You're right, I am too close to this. Thank you."

Sophia cleared her throat, thinking of how to broach the subject of regressing Cathy again.

Her colleague raised her head and met Sophia's gaze. "Is there something you want to share?"

"I know you aren't too hip on continuing your regressions to see what happened in that lifetime during the Great Depression, but I really think this is all interrelated," said Sophia, gesturing to the paper on her desk.

Cathy sighed. "As crazy as it seems, somehow that sounds right." She sat up in the chair. "When are you available?"

"I'm meeting with Gerald shortly, but I could this afternoon or evening."

"How about this afternoon. I'd like to get to the bottom of this as soon as possible. And speaking of Gerald, how is he doing? Any luck with his snake fear?"

Sophia gave her a wry smile. "His situation is a lot like yours at the moment. We've opened Pandora's box in terms of significant past lifetimes, and now everything is coming out, snakes and all."

As if on cue, the front door chimed.

Cathy stood. "Well, I feel for him." She was about to turn, but then gave Sophia a quizzical look. "I can't help but think I'm experiencing all of this with my past lifetime so that I can see what we're really looking at in terms of taking on more of the work here at the center. Do you think my theory has any merit?"

"Definitely."

They left the room, Cathy going down the hallway to her office, while Sophia made her way to the waiting room, where she found Gerald pouring himself a cup of coffee.

"Good morning, Dr. Strand," he said, then blew on the hot liquid and took a tentative sip.

Sophia appraised him, noting that he appeared even more tired than the day before.

Once they had settled themselves in her office, Sophia asked, "Any new developments since we spoke this morning?"

"May has texted me several times that her father still hasn't shown up." He put the coffee on the side table. "I haven't answered her yet. She won't take my advice about contacting the police, so I'm all out of suggestions."

"Let's start the regression. Maybe things will be clearer when we're done as to how you should respond."

Gerald nodded and yawned. "Fair warning, I barely slept last night. I may just pass out."

Sophia smiled. "It just so happens the best regressions often occur when someone is very tired, so you're in luck."

Gerald looked at her with chagrin. "Luck is something I could do with right about now. That and clarity."

"I think you just might find both," said Sophia, who turned on the sound of light rain and began the meditation.

Chapter Twenty Two

Devan sped through a tunnel, crouching as he ran. It was tight in here, but he had learned to contort and compress his body while in the cage. All he knew was that he needed to get to Lan before they found her and tortured her, or worse. His side ached and his feet felt like they were on fire, but he pressed on.

After he had rescued Lan's father and stabbed the guard, Devan had run from the tent toward the tunnel. It was during training that he learned about the system of underground tunnels created two decades prior by the Vietnamese—an insurance policy in case they found themselves at war. He had seen a soldier climb up out of the tunnel when he'd been watching the tent where they held Hieu.

Devan arrived at a sharp turn in the tunnel then and came face-to-face with an impasse. Part of the tunnel had fallen into the path, a pile of rocks now blocking his way. He began scrabbling to remove rocks so that he could pass, but stopped when he heard shifting from above. He took a deep breath and willed himself to work slowly and methodically, stopping often to ensure conditions remained stable. Finally, he cleared enough that he could climb over the rocks and continue.

Sophia watched as Gerald seemed rushed, his breathing labored. On several occasions, he spoke about a tunnel and getting to Lan. It was evident he had managed to escape the Viet Cong's grasp and was heading to save Lan, AKA May.

When the tunnel ended, Devan looked up to see an opening to the surface and the night sky, still dark. He climbed the side of the tunnel, digging his feet into the soft earth as he ascended. As he pulled himself up and out of the tunnel onto solid ground, he listened intently. No sounds. From what he could tell, he had been heading west toward Lan's hut in the jungle, but it was impossible now to tell if he had overshot her house. He glanced up at the night sky, grateful for the half-moon and bright stars, which would help guide him. Then he closed his eyes and listened again. Still silent. While any other time he would welcome the silence, now it felt oppressive and only reminded him that Lan was in jeopardy as the Viet Cong silently made their way to her.

Sophia checked the clock to see that Gerald had been under for a good thirty minutes. He seemed to be okay, despite somewhat labored breathing. When he was silent for a time, she asked him, "Where are you Devan?"

"I am out of the tunnel but I don't know how to find Lan. If I don't find her soon, I fear I will lose her forever." His expression became pained.

"Listen to your gut," said Sophia then, not sure where the words of advice were coming from. "Your instincts have gotten you this far. Stop and tap into them. They will guide you."

After a few moments of silence, Devan said, "I know which way."

Devan stopped to get his bearings and to realign. He felt an overwhelming urge to head what he believed was east, toward the moon hanging in the sky. He resumed running, ears finely tuned and all senses on overdrive. It was when he reached the edge of the jungle that he stopped to listen intently. Though barely audible, he could hear what appeared to be the murmur of voices. He was just stepping into the jungle when he suddenly felt himself fall, as if into an abyss.

When Gerald yelped, Sophia sat up straighter and asked, "What is happening, Devan?"

"It's not Devan."

"Where are you, Brock?"

"I'm still in the forest. It's nighttime."

"What are you doing?"

"I felt a bad vibe, so I left the cabin and I'm hiding in the woods. I think the fuzz are coming to get me. The people who let me stay in the cabin sold me out."

"What will you do?"

Gerald's face contorted. "What can I do? I've run from my country, and now I'm on the run in another country."

"Some deserters go home. Is that something you would want to do?" asked Sophia.

Gerald squared his shoulders as if to protest, but then let them fall. "I don't know. Maybe. I'm beginning to think facing my punishment may be better than being faceless and on the run for the rest of my life. And I miss Cheryl really bad, man."

Brock remained crouched under the cover of a giant oak, his heart pounding not from exertion but from an overwhelming disdain and repulsion for himself. He put his head in his hands, suppressing the urge to howl out here in the dark. What had his cowardliness gotten him but pain and misery? He rose up and starting walking, this time nearly running into a fallen tree. As he climbed up and over, he felt himself slip into a black hole.

Devan could tell from deep within himself that he neared Lan's hut. He passed a stand of trees he recognized in the dim light. Not too much further and he would be to her. He hoped her father made it back. Then he could get all of them to the demilitarized zone and safety.

As he came upon the hut, he slowed and listened. Silence. Was Lan still asleep and blissfully unaware of what had happened? He crept up and entered, his breath sucked from his body at what he saw.

Chapter Twenty
Three

When Gerald began wailing, a guttural cry that would surely frighten everyone in the office, Sophia said sharply, "I am going to bring you back now. When I count back from ten, you are going to pass through the purple door to the here and now." Ten, nine, eight, seven. Come on back. Six, five, four, three, two, one. You are back in Orange now," said Sophia, who sat at the edge of her seat, her own breathing shallow as Gerald stopped crying out and went mute. He had put his hands over his face and now removed them.

"Gerald, are you okay?"

He continued to stare at the ceiling for several long moments, finally turning to face her. "I know what happened with my Devan self and Lan, who we know is May, and her father. I also saw myself as Brock."

Sophia watched Gerald struggle to compose himself.

"Take your time," she said.

He sat up slowly and his face fell. "I didn't make it to May in time. When I got to their hut, I found them both." He stopped to look down at his hands grasped in his lap, then managed to finish, his voice strangled, "Butchered."

"Oh, my, Gerald, that must have been horrible to see," said Sophia. "What did you do then?"

He swallowed. "I ran to the demilitarized zone to safety."

"Is that something you could have done before?"

"Yes, but I didn't want to leave May."

"So, you stayed with her, despite the danger."

"And in so doing, I put May and her father's lives in danger. My inaction got them killed."

He put his head in his hands. "There's something more. I think though I did make it to safety, I didn't last long after that. The experience destroyed me."

"That would make sense, given the fact that you reincarnated into this lifetime, I'm estimating, in the early 1980s," said Sophia.

"Actually, 1979," said Gerald, who frowned. "Since that inaction got everyone killed in that lifetime, is this my sign to act now?"

Sophia thought about his question. "I think it's part of your answer. You also saw yourself as Brock. What happened with that?"

"I was alone in the woods because the Canadian police had come for me. I felt ashamed for shirking my responsibilities, and I was really lonely. I turned myself in and dealt with the consequences of going AWOL. Do you think that's also my lesson? That I need to face my duties here?"

"Meaning, what?"

"That I need to go help May and her father before they are both harmed?"

Sophia considered her answer, aware that whatever she suggested could be especially dangerous for her client, as well as May and her father.

"I know you said May is against telling the authorities about her father's predicament, but it seems to me that might be the best course of action. In Vietnam you couldn't get help in that manner, but now you can. I think you take advantage of that. And as Brock, you did go to the authorities. I think that might be your lesson. To trust in help from others—in particular those who have the power and resources to help."

Gerald thought for a moment, then nodded. "I have a friend who knows someone in the Westminster police department where May and her father live. I'm going to call him right away, and then I'll go to May." He pulled his phone out of his pocket and checked the screen. "I have several messages from her. Excuse me."

Sophia waited as Gerald checked his messages, his expression becoming increasingly anxious. Then he made another call. When he finished, he said, "May has gone to meet the men holding her father. She only has part of the money with her. I got it out of my deposit box and gave it to her when her father disappeared. But only having partial payment puts her in grave danger. My friend is going to meet me at the Westminster PD. I'm sorry to rush out."

"No need to apologize. Please go. My prayers will be with May and her father."

After he left, Sophia sat down at her desk to think through the last couple of hours. While everything that had transpired seemed to make sense, something kept niggling at her about Gerald's past parallel lifetime.

"You look deep in thought," said Cathy from the doorway. "I heard Gerald leave. How did that go?"

"I'm not sure," said Sophia.

Cathy walked into the room, her eyebrows raised. "You're usually so sure about things. This is unlike you."

Sophia stared over Cathy's shoulder at her fountain. "Everything seems so—I don't know how to explain it. Unhinged right now. As if I'm missing a critical piece of Gerald's puzzle."

Cathy sat down in the chair opposite Sophia, her expression concerned. "I'm not sure what's going on here, Sophia. Are you okay?"

Sophia shook her head to clear it. "Gerald's regression was pretty intense. I know we had talked about me checking out that insurance notice and doing a regression on you, but first, I need to see Phillip's notes. Is it possible we could do that right now?"

Cathy, still looking concerned, nodded slowly. "Sure, but before we do, perhaps you should have something to eat? You don't look too good right now. Could be a blood sugar thing."

"Let's stop for fast food."

Cathy patted the arms of the chair she sat in several times, as if doing so would right the room. "That's a great idea. Let's go. I'll drive."

After going through a drive-through for hamburgers, they went to Cathy's house in Tustin, where she parked in the driveway, then turned to Sophia. "You feeling any better? You've been quiet all the way here."

"Don't worry about me. I'm fine. This can happen with the past life work. You sometimes need to do some digging. It's kind of like detective work."

Cathy shook her head. "The more I see of what you do with these past life cases, the more convinced I am that we're going to need to charge more than the standard rates. This is heavy duty stuff."

Sophia gave a short laugh. "I'm glad to see that this hasn't scared you off yet."

Cathy picked up the bag of burgers and reached for the car door handle. "You know that us Farrows are made of stern stuff. This whole thing would have energized and excited my brother. I can at least give it a try."

Once inside, Cathy insisted they eat first. When they finished, she led Sophia to the back of the house, where she pulled a ladder from the ceiling just as her phone rang. She checked the screen. "I've got to get this. Go ahead on up. Chuck pulled the boxes out last night. Excuse me."

Sophia climbed up into the musty-smelling attic where the afternoon sun revealed dust motes suspended in the air. She went to the boxes in the center of the room and knelt next to them to see they were all labeled by subject.

"You're here Phillip. I can feel you," said Sophia then. "I hope you've come to help me understand this parallel life situation of Gerald's. Please show me what I'm missing."

"Find the last physics class I taught before I went to Iraq," he said.

Sophia checked the dates on the sides of the boxes, locating the one he spoke of and pulling it toward her. As she began removing documents with Phillip's handwriting, her heart tugged. She stopped to hold a sheath of papers to her chest, recalling those final days before he went to Iraq. How he seemed to be putting his affairs in order, though he kept insisting he'd be back.

"Those days before you left for Iraq. You knew you wouldn't be coming back, didn't you? That's why you labeled all of this? Isn't it?"

Phillip didn't answer for a time, then finally said, "I did suspect, yes."

"But you promised me you would be fine. You lied." Tears started to form at the back of Sophia's eyes, and she willed them to remain at bay.

"But I was fine. I went into the Light where I've been since I left you. It's you that wasn't fine, but now you are. You've lived a wonderful life, and now you have a new love."

Sophia put the sheath of papers on her lap. "My new love has a few wrinkles I'm not so sure about, but maybe you know that."

"I've been true to my word and haven't been eavesdropping, but I did tell you Ryan has had his own share of heartache. Heartache that you will be able to help him with when the time is right."

Sophia looked out of the portal window to see the sky darkening, which cast a gray light into the attic. She stood up and pulled on a light, illuminating the space.

"I'm not sure I have the strength for anymore heartache," she said then, her voice barely a whisper.

"I urge you to give Ryan a chance, my love. This was meant to be. Now let's focus on the matter at hand. Take a look at my notes."

Sophia began riffling through the papers, which contained a variety of physics theories. It was when she came to a theory about the idea of time stretching, shrinking, and morphing to allow in new experiences and to remove them that she stopped. This passage, dated a month before his passing, was written in Phillip's hand, and had no references to texts by famous physicists like the other notes. As she read the theory, her breathing quickened.

"This is yours, Phillip," she said when she finished. "A theory that no one else has seen, isn't it?"

"Yes, my love."

Sophia put her hand on the text, her heart beating hard now. "This explains how the parallel lifetimes are possible, doesn't it? Time can stretch and morph, as you say here, so that various realities have a place to exist within the constructs of time," she said, reading a portion of what he had written. "But the purpose of the parallel lifetimes? What is that?"

"You know the answer," said Phillip. "Think about it."

Sophia closed her eyes and thought about Gerald and his journey as Devan and Brock. "The parallel lifetimes are meant to complement one another while at the same time they are mirroring one another," she said. "They are meant to teach the soul two lessons at the same time—lessons that mirror one another and complement one another. Lessons that expand the soul exponentially. Much more so than it could be expanded with the one lesson."

"Bravo, my love. And what more? I know you see it."

Sophia gulped over the lump that had formed in her throat. "They are meant to show a soul the depths of the soul. They are meant to foster self-love and love of others. That's the overriding lesson, isn't it?"

"As I said, you knew the answer all along," said Phillip.

"For Gerald this is all about love—this journey."

Just then, Cathy appeared at the top of the ladder. "I hear you talking. Have you figured things out?"

Sophia nodded. "I have. Excuse me. I need to make a quick call."

Cathy nodded. "I'll be downstairs."

The phone rang several times before Gerald answered. When he did, his voice sounded strained.

"Gerald, how are things going?"

"The police believe they know where May and her father are, and they're going to breach soon. It's a rough part of town, and they warned me that they might not still be alive."

"Listen to me carefully. This may sound strange and as if it won't help, but if you admit to yourself your love for May, I think she will make it out unscathed," said Sophia.

Gerald was quiet for a moment. "It's funny you should say that. Just a little while ago, something came over me and I realized I love her, and that I always have. From the moment we met again in this lifetime, I've known it. I was just afraid of it until now. I promised myself if she makes it out that I'm going to give us a chance."

Sophia smiled. "I'm glad to hear that, Gerald. I wish you the best and pray for her and her father's safe return. Please keep me posted."

After she hung up the phone, Sophia sent a text to Ryan. *Thinking about you. I hope you are holding up okay. I'm here if you need me.* Then she signed off with a heart emoji.

Chapter
Twenty Four

When Sophia came down from the attic with the box in tow, she asked Cathy, "Can I borrow these?"

Her sister-in-law waved her hand. "Keep them. They are gibberish to me. All they'll do is turn to dust up there. I hope they were helpful?"

"Very, thank you." She looked to see that Cathy had the liability insurance paperwork in front of her on the kitchen table.

"I decided to call about this while I was waiting, and you were right, it was a clerical error," she told Sophia. "I'd love to know how you knew that, but I'm even more eager to do my past life regression. That is if you're still up for it."

"I'm definitely up for it. I think the best place to do the regression is in the office. Did you want to head back?"

Cathy sprang up. "Now that my mind is more at ease about things, I'm ready. Let's go."

Thirty minutes later, Sophia had Cathy in a meditative state and ready to walk through the purple door.

"I don't know if I want to see how far we fell," she said.

"You could find that you fared well. And if you didn't, remember that was then and this is now."

Cathy sighed. "Okay, I'm going in."

For a few moments, she said nothing. Then she exclaimed, her face beaming, "Bradford's Benz. It's back to pristine condition. Even better than before."

"That sounds promising. What else do you see, and who is there?"

"Madeline is here with her little girl, who is now six. She's adorable, and I've just given her some clothing I made at the shop."

"You have a shop?"

Cathy smiled. "Yes, it's a lovely little place. I didn't want anything too overwhelming. I just wanted a small place to create and produce. We were able to buy the shop at a song with money we socked away during the Depression. We sold all the cars but the Benz, which helped us dig our way out."

"It sounds like you're happy," said Sophia.

Cathy's smile was broad now. "We are. We're going to celebrate my birthday later today when we close the shop. This time it'll be a small family affair, but it makes me so happy."

"What do you think your lesson is from this?" Sophia asked her.

"That I don't need bigger and grander. All I need is what makes my heart sing. I know what I'm going to wish for when I blow out the candles this time."

"What are you going to wish for?"

"Simplicity and a happy heart," said Cathy.

"It sounds like you have that. Would you like to come back to the now?"

Cathy shook her head. "I think there is something I need to see up ahead. Several years ahead."

Sophia's interest piqued, she asked, "How many years ahead?"

"The year 2030."

Sophia wasn't sure about this. "Maybe it would be better just to let 2030 come to you in its own time."

"I need to see."

Sophia sighed. "Okay, go ahead and head back through the purple door and head down the path." Suddenly, Sophia saw a turquoise-colored door. "Head through the door to the future and tell me what you see."

Cathy appeared hesitant at first but then said, "I just opened the door." Then her expression became serious.

"Did you walk through?"

She shook her head. "No, I saw something I don't like. I closed the door. You're right. It's best I don't go any further."

"Okay, I want you to walk down the path toward the now. I'm going to count down from ten. When I reach one, you'll be back home in Orange, 2022."

When Cathy opened her eyes and sat up a few minutes later, she said, "It turned out alright for us, didn't it? I opened a great little shop. And Madeline was there with her cute little girl." She chuckled. "I did ask her the other day if there was any chance she could be pregnant and she proceeded to explain to me that with how busy work is, she doesn't have time to sleep, let alone have a relationship, so her being pregnant at this time isn't a possibility."

"But it likely will be in the future. It could be you got a glimpse of your future granddaughter," said Sophia.

Cathy smiled widely. "Well, she's a cutie!" Then she frowned. "Did something else happen?"

Sophia thought about the final peek behind the turquoise door and made an executive decision not to mention it. Cathy hadn't said what she'd seen, and what good would it do for her to worry about eight years in the future?

"I think your main lesson is that things worked out then with your business and they can work out now, providing you follow your heart."

Sophia found the section of the tape where Cathy spoke about following her heart and played it for her.

When she finished listening, Cathy said, "That answers my questions about where to go with the practice. We can continue to service insurance clients with the one company we're still contracted with, but I want to do a big push for cash clients. I've done the math. With the increase in what we'll be paid with cash, minus taxes, we need half as many traditional clients. And then we can add the past life clients. What do you think? I know it's risky, but are you okay with going rogue?"

"I like the idea—especially the part about no longer having to fill out reams of paperwork only to be paid a pittance months later. I'm also thrilled about expanding the past life work. I know it will be a bit overwhelming and will involve a learning curve for you, but I really think it can help people."

"It's settled then," said Cathy, who looked out the window at the stormy weather. "How about we go to my house and celebrate. You up for that? We can talk about how we can begin adding more past life work. And how you're going to teach me all I need to know."

Sophia stood and went to her bookcase. "Your first assignment is to read this book." She handed Cathy *Many Lives, Many Masters.*

"I will do that right away. Then we can discuss?"

"Definitely," said Sophia.

Later that night after Sophia returned to her condo, she saw Teddy's backpack next to his door in the hallway, the lights off in his room. She went into the kitchen to get a glass of water when her phone lit up. It was Ryan calling.

"Hi, Ryan, it's late there. Is everything okay?" Sophia knew as soon as the words escaped her mouth what had happened.

"My mother passed a little while ago."

"I'm so sorry, Ryan. Are you okay?"

"It has been tough on everyone, especially my dad. But she was in such pain. It was almost a relief."

"I understand that. I felt the same when my mother passed."

"Thank you for saying that, and for being there for me," said Ryan. "It has been a very long time since I had someone I could talk to. To be honest, I don't think I've ever had someone like you I could talk to."

At the weight of his words, Sophia felt a rush of something she couldn't quite pinpoint, but it felt good, settling somewhere in her middle and giving her a profound sense of peace and contentment.

"I'm really glad I can be here for you. And I feel the same in terms of having someone I can talk to," she said.

"It was meant to be, wasn't it, us meeting?" His words were more of a statement than a question.

"I believe so, yes."

"I wish I could stay on the phone with you all night, but I need to go thank the pastor for coming here in the middle of the night to send her off. Thank you for answering Sophia."

When they hung up, the wavy form of a woman appeared in front of Sophia. She looked like Ryan. "Thank you. He is going to need you," she said.

Jake's mother flashed through Sophia's mind then and she started to ask about her, but the figure had vanished.

"All will make sense in time, and you will be fine with this," said Sophia's life guide Athena then. "You are well equipped for this next chapter with Ryan. You'll see."

Sophia sat there for some time in the quiet of the night listening to the clock tick and thinking about how time marched on and yet time stood still. Though she had some trepidation about the next leg of her journey, she had to admit to herself that not knowing how things might unfold with Ryan enticed and excited her.

Epilogue

It was two days before Gerald called.

"Dr. Strand, forgive the delay in getting back to you, but it has been quite a whirlwind."

"How did things turn out with May and her father?"

"I am so glad that I took your advice and contacted the police. Her father was moments away from being executed by the people he owed money to, and May's fate may have been much worse. The men were all arrested and are likely to end up in prison for a long time."

"I'm so happy to hear that. Thank goodness everyone is safe," said Sophia.

"There is a lot to still figure out. May's father has agreed to get help for his gambling addiction, and she and I..." He cleared his throat. "May and I have decided to give our relationship a chance. I should probably say that I have decided, because she was never hesitant about it. I'm still a bit uncomfortable about the age difference but knowing she and I have been together over many lifetimes does make that aspect much easier to accept."

"It sounds like you're happy," said Sophia.

"I am. I feel more in alignment than I ever have, which is good, given what I teach people."

"And your seminar?"

"That's tomorrow. Although I'm not as prepared as I usually am, I feel more prepared than I ever have, if that makes any sense at all."

"It makes perfect sense. I must ask, however, since it's why you came to me in the first place. What about your fear of snakes?"

"Oh, I forgot to tell you. I think I'm cured. May and I went to a local herbal shop in Little Saigon, and the owner happened to have a snake in a terrarium. Usually, I would have run straight out of the shop, but I was able to go up and take a look at the snake without panicking. I'm not going to say that I'd be happy to pick it up or anything, but the overpowering terror and sheer anxiety I once had is gone."

"I had some time to think through your experience and the fear of snakes over the last few days as I compiled my notes," said Sophia. "As you likely know, the snake is used as a symbol for medicine and the medical profession. It appears to me that your snake fear was symbolic of the need to unlock and heal that lifetime, and it led you to do so."

"Wow, I never thought of that, Dr. Strand. But what about my alternate life as Brock?"

"Your experience has caused me to study parallel existences in more detail. From what I can see looking at your dual lifetimes, your Brock self gave into fear and ran only to find himself alone and wishing that he had embraced the fear and his destiny."

"In a way, I did that with May at first. Initially I wanted to run from her."

"That's true, you did. I've found that after the regression therapy, more pieces of the puzzle usually begin to fall together. You will likely continue to get epiphanies for some time," said Sophia.

"I'll be sure to let you know what comes up. Before you go, I have a request. My sister would like to see you. I recently shared with her what occurred with my treatment, and she said she has a past life she would like to unravel. It involves someone she has reconnected with. I suspect a former boyfriend. She and her husband separated a few months ago."

"I'll be happy to talk to your sister."

"Thank you for that and for everything, Dr. Strand. I'll be eternally grateful to you. I also suspect that past lives will be making their way into my next book."

Sophia laughed. "That I look forward to reading."

Two weeks later, Gerald's sister, Bridgette, came to see Sophia. She had made the appointment soon after Sophia and Gerald had spoken, but canceled twice before finally making it in.

"Hopefully the third time is the charm," said the woman, a perky redhead, who stood a good foot shorter than her brother. She wore jeans and an emerald green blouse and had her shoulder length hair pulled back in a ponytail.

"It's very nice to meet you, and I'm sure the third time is the charm," said Sophia.

Bridgette grinned. "I know I look nothing like Gerald. I take more after my mother, and he got my father's good looks."

"Would you like some coffee or water?"

Bridgette patted her canvas handbag, decorated in corgis. "I've got a water bottle, so I'm good."

"Cute purse. Do you like dogs?"

Bridgette beamed. "I love them—especially my two corgis."

Once they were in Sophia's office, with Bridgette seated across from her desk, she leaned back in her chair and said, "Your brother tells me you've recently reconnected with someone with whom you believe you have had a past lifetime?"

Bridgette's once sunny disposition faded and her expression became anxious. "Yes, he's a prior boyfriend. I kind of ran away from the relationship, and I didn't think I'd ever see him again."

"But now you have. I must ask, was he violent with you?"

Bridgette looked at her purse, then back at Sophia. "I'm really embarrassed to say this."

Sophia nodded for her to continue.

The woman held up her hands as if surrendering. "I just want you to know that this is nothing like me. I mean, I haven't ever done anything like this in my entire life. Except with him."

"That is generally indicative of a past lifetime issue," said Sophia.

Bridgette's expression became more animated. "That's what I was thinking. When Gerald told me about his experience, I just kept wondering, is that the case with Razz and me?"

"His name is Razz?"

"That's the nickname I gave him. His real name is John, but I used to razz him about what a boring name that is, so one day I told him that I would call him Razz." Bridgette's face reddened then.

"So, has Razz harmed you verbally or physically?"

Now Bridgette's face was a deep red. "That's just the thing, it's not him, it's me."

"Meaning?"

Bridgette let out a big breath. "Meaning it's me who has been verbally abusive, and sometimes physically, too."

This surprised Sophia. "Has this been the case with your relationship from the beginning?"

Bridgette looked out the window for a moment without answering.

"What you say here won't go any further," Sophia assured her.

Bridgette looked Sophia in the eyes. "I don't know what comes over me when I'm with Razz, but I'm not very nice. I don't like myself when I'm with him. That's why I moved across the country to get away from him."

"You're not a tall woman," said Sophia. "I don't mean that as an offense, but I'm thinking that the times you have been physically abusive with him, he has let you?"

Bridgette wiped tears from her eyes. "Yes, and that makes me even more mad. I'm telling you; this is crazy on so many levels.

He's actually a really nice guy. Much nicer than my soon-to-be ex-husband."

As Bridgette said this, Sophia saw her with two men, then the vision disappeared as quickly as it came.

"From what you are telling me, this sounds like a past life issue. If we do some regressions, we'll find out why you have this paradigm with Razz. It sounds to me that if your feelings were to change about him, there might be a chance for a good relationship?"

Bridgette nodded vigorously. "Yes, he checks all the boxes for me. And I'm not always upset with him. Sometimes we get along really well. It's as if I become possessed at times, though. I tell my girlfriends about how he irritates me for no reason at all, and they think I'm absolutely bonkers."

"Past lifetime effects on current lifetimes are very complex, but I've had great success helping people get to the crux of things and make 360-degree differences," said Sophia.

"I'm ready for a change. Do you think you can help me?"

"I can certainly try."

See what happens with Bridgette in *Suspended Control.*

A Note For You

Dear Reading Gem,

Thanks for spending time with me and Sophia!

Past lives collide with current lifetimes in The Past Life Prism Series Time Travel Suspense. Starring Sophia Strand, a past life regression therapist, the series chronicles the torrid tales of significant relationships spanning centuries. Watch romance kindled, sparks fly, and intrigue unveiled as couples reunite in present day.

If you like this book, please leave a review or just stars on Amazon, GoodReads, and/or BookBub. Your opinion matters and is incredibly powerful.

Thanks again and talk soon!

Julie

Stay Enlightened

Thanks for reading! Let's stay in touch. I post insider information, and sneak peeks of upcoming books on my website at https://www.juliebawdendavis.com/fiction. You can also email me at Julie@JulieBawdenDavis.com, find me on Facebook, and follow me on Amazon.

Even better, join my weekly VIP Reading Gems news-letter here. When signing up, you get a free copy of *Discovered Beginnings*, the prequel novella to my Discovered Truth Series. There are also lots of giveaways and contests!

Escape to Unforgettable Romance and Intrigue...

Books by Julie Bawden-Davis

The Past Life Prism Series
(Romantic Time Travel Suspense)
Suspended: The Beginning
Suspended Enforcement
Suspended Entrapment
Suspended Exodus
Suspended Entanglement
The Past Life Prism Series Box Set: Books 1-4
Suspended Control

The Discovered Truth Series
(Romantic Suspense)
Discovered Beginnings:
(FREE at https://www.juliebawdendavis.com/fiction)
Discovered Secrets
Discovered Memories
Discovered Indiscretions
Discovered Liaisons
Discovered Betrayal
Discovered Denial
Discovered Distractions

BOOKS BY JULIE BAWDEN-DAVIS

Discovered Deception
Discovered Lies
Discovered Vengeance
Discovered Redemption
Discovered Obsession
Discovered Transgressions
Discovered Suspicion
Discovered Escape
Discovered Promises
Discovered Cover-Up
Discovered Intentions

www.ingramcontent.com/pod-product-compliance
Lightning Source LLC
Chambersburg PA
CBHW022021170626
46808CB00003B/1008